# THIRTY-SEVEN

# THIRTY-SEVEN

## a novel

## PETER STENSON

**DZANC BOOKS**

**DZANC BOOKS**

5220 Dexter Ann Arbor Rd.
Ann Arbor, MI 48103
www.dzancbooks.org

Library of Congress Cataloging-in-Publication Data

Names: Stenson, Peter, author.
Title: Thirty-seven : a novel / by Peter Stenson.
Description: Ann Arbor, MI : Dzanc Books, [2017]
Identifiers: LCCN 2017003745 | ISBN 9781945814310
Classification: LCC PS3619.T4764777 T48 2017 | DDC 813/.6--dc23
LC record available at https://lccn.loc.gov/2017003745

First US edition: February 2018
Interior design by Michelle Dotter

Printed in the United States of America

10   9   8   7   6   5   4   3   2   1

"Truth is like the sun. You can shut it out for a time, but it ain't goin' away."

—Elvis Presley

# 1. MODUS PONENS

One always said sickness bears Honesty. I'm not sure if I agree with him. Sometimes I think sickness bears more sickness.

This story isn't about Dr. James Shepard, whom I knew as One.

I wasn't given a name at birth. I was given one three weeks later, when I was adopted. It's Mason Hues. You haven't heard of me. For a year, I went by Thirty-Seven. Sometimes I think numbers are a better representation of our true selves because they denote the order in which we arrived.

One always said survivors were the only people worthy of living. He said that a person is a prisoner to the idea of *betterment* until he cannot see a single thing left worth living for. He said that nobody is grateful when he's enslaved to the entitled notion of things improving.

I'm eighteen years old. This number is perhaps more important than anything else. It means I'm now a man, now able to die for this country. It means my record is now sealed, any crimes expunged. It means had I been eighteen thirty months ago, I would more than likely be doing life, like the rest of my family.

One always said that if somebody tells you a story isn't about something, it sure as hell is.

I ran away when I was fifteen. This wasn't because I was un-loved or abused—although more than once, I awoke to the man who swore to love and protect me standing in my doorway, the rhythmic rustling of him pleasuring himself to my sleeping body an unmistakable type of gong—and it wasn't because I was steeped in want of anything in particular. I grew up wealthy. I grew up in private schools. I had enough friends. I ran away because every-thing seemed easy. Too easy, fake.

One always said that Honesty bears change. I agree with this. The very nature of Honesty calls for change. Its presence won't al-low for anything else. Once something is known, it fundamentally alters those who know it. It forces action, even if that action is *inaction*.

This story isn't about sex. It's not about love. It's not even about family.

I was the thirty-seventh person to knock on the doors of Dr. James Shepard's Colorado estate in search of something real. That's what I honestly believed I was searching for: *realness*. Maybe I was. I was young, fifteen, like I said. Maybe I was simply searching for shelter. Maybe I was leaving one adopted home for another. Maybe I was searching for *betterment*. Maybe I thought it my right as a person with a name to choose my own abusive father.

Dr. Turner worked with me at CMHIP[1] to alter my use of pro-nouns. She inflicted small punishments for my incessant use of *we*. Sometimes she wouldn't let me play four square. Other times she wouldn't allow me to have books in my room. I was congratulated the first time I said *I*: I want you all to leave me alone.

One said the use of acronyms was a tool of shirking Honesty. He said POW was comical coming out of a person's mouth, juvenile, even fun. He said *Prisoner of War* didn't have the same placating

---

1 CMHIP—Colorado Mental Health Institute at Pueblo

effect. He said that as humans, everything we did was in order to bury, obstruct, and alter Truth.

I remember learning the concept of modus ponens in ninth-grade math class. It's an antiquated rule of inference. It states that if P implies Q, and P is true, then Q is true. One said that sickness bears Honesty. He said Honesty bears change. Therefore, sickness bears change. It's really as simple as that.

This story isn't about ideas. It's not about ideals. It's not about betterment.

I live in a studio apartment in Denver, Colorado. It's Section 8 housing. I haven't spoken to my adopted parents in over three years. I eat rice and drink Mr. Pibb for every meal. I spent thirty months in adolescent correctional facilities, both penal and mental health. My record is clean. Nobody knows me as Thirty-Seven.

One's favorite singer was Elvis. I know every song by heart. Crying into a five-gallon painter's bucket, my teeth disintegrating underneath their constant coating of acidic bile, will forever remind me of "Blue Moon."

The three deepest, most telling, and unflappable aspects of a person's character are his first love, his favorite memory, and his deepest regret. When I was fifteen, I spoke these into One's ear. For the life of me, I cannot remember what I told him. But looking back, that moment—the granite boulder digging into my legs, the stars like a child kleptomaniac obsessed with things that sparkle, the warmth radiating from a stranger's neck—now encapsulates all three character-determining aspects.

I have wants now. I want a box spring. I want one of those razors that jiggle to ensure the closest shave. I want a significant other. Someday, I'd like to learn to drive, so I guess I'd like a car. A bicycle would do for now. I've learned it's okay to have material wants; they are not inherently selfish.

We were survivors. That's what you know us as: The Survivors. It was never to be our name because we'd shed our names, our origins of birth, our shackles to wanting beings perpetuating the bullshit cycle of consumerism in order to stave off mortality. We were One and Five and Thirty-Seven. We were survivors because we endured round after round of chemotherapy. Some of us didn't. Twenty-Two died of phenomena. Thirty-One died of an infection. Of course, you know about the ones who died on February tenth.

This story isn't about voluntarily going through chemo. It's not about Survivors, at least not with a capital S. It's not about family members who died.

I'm eighteen. I used to be Thirty-Seven. I used to be Mason Hues. I used to be John Doe.

One always said that consequences were 99.9% man-made. I found this difficult to believe until we did things without the world's judgmental eyes, and then I understood his words to be true.

Dr. Turner told me in CMHIP that I could be anything I wanted. She told me my entire life lay ahead of me. She told me I was smart, exceptionally so. She told me I could go to college and pick my profession. She asked me, if I could choose anything, what I wanted to be when I grew up. I thought for a second and then answered, making sure to use the first person singular: I want to be anonymous in a group of people who've nursed me through my pleas for death.

This story isn't about what happened on February tenth. It's not about The Day of Gifts. It's not about the seventy-seven people who were murdered.

I was fifteen when I ran away. I was fifteen when One put a needle in my arm and shot me with my first dose of Cytoxan. I was fifteen when I was arrested and charged with seventy-seven counts of being an accessory to murder. I was fifteen when I lost my name once again, the authorities keeping me anonymous. Just a token of horror for the masses to rally behind, a child in the wrong place at the wrong time. Poor kid, poor fucking kid.

One also said that if somebody explicitly tells you what a story is about, to keep your heart closed because this person was preaching, and nothing—not a single damn thing—coming out of a preacher's mouth is ever True.

One always said we are nothing without one another. He said everything could be traced back to the loneliness of our family of origin's cruelties of abandonment. He said we were doing the most remarkable thing imaginable: forging bonds deeper than blood, embarking upon lives free of want amidst a loving family of our own choosing.

This story is about a boy who ran away from adopted parents who loved him the best they knew how. It's about a boy who found a home in the mountains of Colorado. It's about a boy who lost his name through three rounds of chemotherapy, his only sickness rooted in the *I*. It's about February tenth, The Day of Gifts. It's about coming of age in locked cells, some with padded walls and some with toilets that never fully got clean. It's about turning eighteen and becoming a man and amassing the small luxuries of even the lower class, crossing off wants without any cerebral wherewithal.

Modus ponens. It's a weird thing to remember learning. It deals with how to infer truth. But it's not a law, and that fact is what keeps me awake on a mattress with no box spring wondering.

# 2. EMPLOYMENT

I know how to listen without hearing words and I know how to listen to words without listening to body language and I know how to listen by simply watching the centimeter of skin that connects the ear to the face. It doesn't matter how gifted a person is in deceit: the creasing, stretching, pulling, and wrinkling of this stretch of skin is the most accurate polygraph ever created.

I'm thinking about this while a woman I don't know cuts my hair. She's older, mid-thirties. Her mirror has a picture of a balding man who probably loves football holding a boy with red hair who seems happy enough. I think her name is Stacey. She sees me notice the picture. She takes this as an invitation to tell me about her family.

It's my first haircut in three years. My hair's a lot darker than it's been most of my life, at least the first fifteen years of living. I understand this to be a normal trait of hair growth after extensive chemotherapy treatments.

She asks how I want my hair and I shrug and she places a heavy book in my lap. I flip through. Every picture looks forced, moments where parents wanted their children to matter and then older children who wanted their parents not to matter. There are a lot of turtlenecks.

I turn to see if she's watching me. She is. I see a twenty-something guy speaking on his cell phone outside of the salon. He smokes a cigarette. I like his air of indifference, even if it's an act. I can't remember seeing his particular hairstyle—buzzed short on the sides and long on top, greased back at a slight angle.

"That," I say.

Stacey sees the guy. She grins like the world suddenly makes sense. She wets my hair and starts cutting. She asks about my plans for the day and I tell her to find a job and she takes this as a chance to tell me about the economy and recession and about her political views.

I also know how to listen while staring into somebody's eyes, giving all the appropriate cues, while not hearing a single word uttered. I'm doing this. The sick know this tactic. So do the incarcerated. My hair falls to the floor. I'd cried the first time I woke up and my sheets were covered in my own poisoned hair. They were tears of joy, of belonging.

Stacey tells me I will have to beat the girls off with a stick. I blush because I'm not good with flirtation. She says, "If you were a few years older..."

"You'd what?"

It's Stacey's turn to blush.

It serves her right. Embarrassment is a passive-aggressive tool used by those who don't believe their wants are worthy of being heard. It's cowardice. If she wants to make a pass at me, she could simply ask if I wanted to copulate in the back of her minivan, the one her balding husband still makes payments on. I would tell her *no*. I would tell her I was a virgin, at least in regard to vaginal intercourse. I would tell her I appreciated her honesty.

"Oh, I'm just kidding around," Stacey says. She runs a comb through my hair. I can see my ears. They look bigger than I remember, longer. Sometimes I wonder if I look more like my maternal mother or father. I wonder how old they were. I wonder if either of their character-defining regrets is giving me up.

"Saying you're probably a real lady-killer, is all," Stacey says. I understand she is trying to do her job. She's paid to cut strangers' hair. She combats her insecurities with dull banter and flirtation. I wonder how many times she's cheated on her husband. I wonder if she has ever done things to harm her son in order to regain a sense of Self. I'm granted no Gifts of Understanding about her outside life because I'm three years removed from living in Honesty. I tell her thanks and she's quiet and the skin connecting her ears slackens. I give her a three-dollar tip, which I think is more than generous.

I live in a part of Denver my parents wouldn't have let me visit alone back when I resided underneath their roof. It's close to The Salvation Army and The Mission, so it's mostly those types of people, at least on the street. But it's gentrifying. There are bars and dispensaries now and even a few music venues. There are a lot of people who look like they're trying very hard to appear poor with their garish tattoos and tight jeans. During the weekends, drunk guys stumble around and scream and try to convince semi-conscious girls to share a cab.

It's okay.

It's fine.

It's all I can realistically ask for.

I stop in a coffee shop and wait in line for six minutes and ask the guy with a neck-beard if they are hiring and he tells me *no*. I go to a deli and am told the same thing. I find a pizza parlor and ask for an application and the girl laughs and tells me it's all done online and I feel stupid but only a little. One always said rejection could either be rooted in fear of fact—either something about you unnerved the other; they were afraid you'd take something they had or prevent them from achieving something they wanted—or fact itself: you weren't good enough.

I walk into a thrift shop on the way to my apartment. I have a good feeling inside the store because a female country singer's doing a cover of "In the Ghetto." The store is cluttered and warm and mildly cared for. I finger the sleeves of shirts. I pick up a pair of black boots with three-inch heels. I'm not sure if they are men's or women's. It seems like the type of store that has cats. I walk over to some men's shirts.

"That shirt would look good on you."

I look over my shoulder. There's a girl around my age, probably a few years older. She's dressed like she needs attention in white and black leggings and a T-shirt with cut-off sleeves, the holes of which expose her naked side ribs and black bra. Her hair is black and boy-short with wisps of sideburns.

"This is normally when you say something," she says.

"Thank you."

"I wasn't complimenting *you*. That shirt would look rad on anybody."

I laugh. So does she. I look down at the shirt. It's solid navy with white snap buttons. She inches toward me and then she's at my side and I feel nervous. She takes the shirt off the rack. She holds it to my chest. The back of her right hand grazes my chin. I think about One cupping my face as he pressed his forehead to mine, our eyes open, us staring into each other's whites, our pupils out of the way so no deception was able to occur.

"Just like I thought. Looks good," she says.

"How much?"

"You don't want to try it on? You're just going to take my word?"

"I guess."

She lowers her hand. She tilts her head. Her neck's skinny and it looks like she has an Adam's apple or maybe that's just because she has short hair and looks a little like a boy.

"You're new, huh?"

"To Denver?"

"Sure."

"I've come back after some time away."

"During your time away, did you learn to speak like a robot?" She smiles. Her teeth are mostly straight like she'd had braces but not worn her retainer.

"Kind of."

"What's in the bag?" She doesn't wait for me to respond and pulls the edge of the King Soopers plastic bag and peeks inside at my two applications. She frowns at me. "That's like the saddest thing I've ever seen." She peeks one more time. "God, it's…Little Johnny out in the big city trying to find a job with his little grocery bag."

I'm not sure what to say so I smile because that's what humans do.

"I just want to fold you up and put you in my change pocket."

"Are you hiring?"

"Are you even old enough to work? To be walking around by yourself, unsupervised?"

"I'm eighteen."

"Let me see your driver's license."

"I don't have one."

"Now I know you're full of shit."

"I don't drive."

Her smile fades and then it's that fake pitying look or maybe it's real pity and she puts her hands on my shoulders and I have to fight from making a sound.

"Be straight with me: who *are* you?"

Her hands are warm through my T-shirt. I want to press my forehead to hers. I want to be back inside. I want to be getting sick while a family member rubbed my back. I never want this moment to end.

"Just a kid looking for a job," I say.

Her chin tries to hide a scar the size of an ant. I tell myself to quit with my own insecurities and wants and focus on hers: she wants something different. She wants what I'd wanted. She comes from money (the confidence evident in her ribbing and her mostly straight teeth), and she's come to Denver for college, where she's probably a sophomore, working here for extra money, but more for something to do that's different from her beer-drinking, morning-after-pill-swallowing friends. She wants authenticity, which she thinks will bring her closeness, the opposite of her family and their fake smiles.

She says, "Are you a good worker?"

"I've never had a job."

"Jesus, you aren't making this easy."

"I imagine I'm a good worker."

"I can give you like two shifts a week, tops twelve hours. No benefits. Shitty pay. But you'll get to play with clothes."

She winks. I smile. I say, "Do I have to talk to your manager or something?"

"Because a girl can't own her own store?"

"No, I mean, I thought…"

"Go ahead and finish that thought, sport."

"You're young," I say.

"Hasn't anybody ever taught you not to judge a book by its cover?" She shakes her head. She points to the sign reading Talley's Tatters. She says, "I'm Talley."

I nod.

"This is where you offer up your name."

The words feel thick in my throat, "Mason Hues."

Talley kind of laughs and shakes her head. "Well, Mason Hues, you have a job, at least a test run to see if it's a good fit. Come in on Thursday. Nine o'clock. Oh, and wear that shirt."

"Yeah?"

"Yeah."

I place the shirt in my plastic bag.

"Once again, now would be the time for a thank you."

"Thank you."

"You may be the most interesting person I've ever met."

"Thank you."

Talley smiles. "I like that you heard that as a compliment."

# 3. WELCOME

Here's the truth about my upbringing: it was good. It was better than good. It was great. My parents loved me and they treated me like I could do no wrong and I played soccer and was good and I kissed a girl and rounded second base during an eighth-grade dance and I felt loved or at least I didn't think about its lack thereof.

My father made money in the tech bubble of the late nineties, selling at the correct time, buying a nice home in Boulder, never really working again. He was a small man, athletic, a cyclist, a lot of strength packed into those sinewy muscles. He read *The Washington Post* every morning. He drank a fair amount, but not alcoholically. He kissed his wife twice a day.

My mother found her second life, post changing diapers, in the industry of betterment. She was an early embracer of yoga and organic foods, a champion of quinoa before everyone knew what it was. She let her hair gray at thirty-six.

Sometimes I think about how hard it must've been for my father. If a person pleasures himself to the sight of his sleeping son, then he obviously has strong pedophilic wants. If he has strong wants, yet doesn't inflict them—at least directly upon his son—he is relying on self-will to keep these desires hidden. Any man acting wholly on self-will is in a constant state of mental, emotional, and spiritual hell. Therefore, my father was in hell. I love him for keeping his transgressions to my doorway.

He had his escapes.

He liked to fly fish.

Or perhaps he liked the *idea* of fly fishing. He liked to sort his gear. He liked to tie his flies with skinned rabbits and quail feathers. He liked to load up his Range Rover and drive up into the mountains and be seen as a rugged outdoorsman instead of a man who retired at thirty-nine. He also liked the notion of me enjoying this activity. I'm sure he envisioned fly fishing as some great bonding experience. I can't blame him for that. He wanted to connect with his son. Perhaps he believed that if he were to develop a closer father-son relationship, the urges would leave, or at least become more taboo.

I was a natural athlete.

I could cast thirty feet on a dime by the time I was seven.

I often out-fished my father. He pretended this made him happy.

I had no interest in catching fish. I had no real interest in nature. I had no interest in gear.

My running away wasn't like you see in the movies. I wasn't addicted to drugs and I wasn't homeless and I wasn't engaging in degradation in order to keep a habit going and food in my stomach. Essentially, my father led me to Dr. James Shepard's massive mountain home. We were out fishing the Crystal, just west of Marble, Colorado. We'd snuck onto private land. My father was a few hundred yards ahead. The browns were biting like they'd never seen a man-made grasshopper. I got bored, as I tended to do. I stared walking up the mountain. I halfheartedly searched for arrowheads. The trees were mostly dead from the mountain pine beetles. I walked for maybe half a mile. I came across a dirt road and figured it was a relic from the days of marble extraction. I followed it for another half mile. That's when I came to a huge home tucked into the western-facing slope of a cliff. It was huge and beautiful, glass windows and cedar logs the size of small cars, angular to help with snowfall.

This was not an uncommon sight. The mountain towns of Colorado were littered with random multimillion-dollar getaways for the Robert Redford types. I walked up to the home. I wondered if there was some small souvenir I could steal for the hell of it. I pressed my face to the glass next to the oversized front door. I saw five or six people, all bald, all skinny, all wearing black scrubs-like outfits. I focused on two sitting on a leather couch, a man and woman, the woman holding the man, the main's face wincing, the woman whispering into his ear, rubbing his chest in circular arcs, this sight the most intimate thing I'd ever witnessed.

A car came crunching down the gravel road. I quickly walked away from the front door. I felt like a trespasser, which I obviously was, but more of the aggressive voyeur type. A black Jeep parked. I didn't have time to hide. The door opened and out stepped a hand-some guy who fit the mold of a mountain man with his canvas Carhartt jacket and dirt-speckled jeans. He wore a wool beanie pushed back on his head. I realized he was *bald*, bald like the others.

He smiled and walked toward me.

I mumbled something about having gotten lost while fishing and accidentally stumbling to his house.

He stopped a few feet away. He was tall, easily six foot three. He said, "Accidents are a way of shirking responsibility."

"I'm sorry, really, I didn't..."

"You did. And that's okay."

He smiled. I wasn't sure if it really was okay. We stood there for an awkward moment. "I should get going," I finally said.

"You remind me of myself when I was your age."

I thought about this man wanting to have sex with me. I wondered who all the people were inside, and why they were all evidently going through chemo.

"Too smart for the world around him. Too stubborn to ask for help. Disenfranchised with the options laid out before him."

"Sorry, again."

He placed his hand on my shoulder. "Never apologize unless you are one hundred percent committed to changing your actions in the future."

"Sorry."

"You did it again."

"I should go."

The man kept his hand on my shoulder. He nodded, which I realized was more of a motion to the house. "They're sick. *We're* sick."

"I'm sorry."

"We're getting better."

"My grandmother beat cancer," I said.

"That's not what's wrong with us."

I turned and glanced back at the house, but I couldn't really see anything from that far away.

"I know you," he said. "I know things come easily for you. I know you have friends. I know you are popular. I know you come from money. I know you are probably out here with your father, who loves you, but not in the way you want. He wouldn't have left you for this long unattended if that weren't true."

He knelt so that his eyes were level with mine.

"But I know you think there is more. More to life. Something with meaning. Something of substance. I know this because people who don't yearn for these things don't walk up to random houses and look in the windows."

I shifted backward. His hand clenched harder on my shoulder. "It's okay. I was like you. They were like you. It's a gift, really." I didn't say anything.

"The knowledge that all of this isn't enough. It just takes the courage to act upon this insight."

"I really should go."

The man let go of my shoulder. He nodded, smiled. He said, "By all means, by all means." I started walking away. That's when he called out. I turned around. He said, "I didn't catch your name."

"Mason."

"I'm One."

"Juan?"

"One, like the number."

"Oh. That's cool."

"You'd be Thirty-Seven."

"Huh?"

"If you ever need to talk, we're here for you."

I'm pretty sure I saw a movie about how a single thought can burrow its way into your mind, germinating with time and experience and want, and grow, the roots mimicking the natural flow of your brain's synapses, first manifesting in dreams, the tentacles breaching your frontal lobe, active thoughts, fantasy creation, the insertion of Self in order to create a version of reality where you're a willing participant of what was now an obsession.

I didn't tell my father about the house in the woods. I didn't tell anyone. I searched online for cancer wards in Marble and didn't find anything. I searched for spiritual retreats and didn't find anything either.[2]

---

2 In CMHIP, Dr. Turner talked to me about various groups' creation myths. She'd say they were designed as a recruiting tool, one with a

---

Three weeks later, a bus brought me to Glenwood Springs. I hiked for four hours and twenty minutes. I sweated and then got cold when the sun set. I found the house. I knocked on the door. The man answered. He extended his arms and hugged me. He said, "Welcome to your life, Thirty-Seven."

---

*loose and broad narrative*, one that invited a person to see himself as the hero, the persecuted, the one being described. She'd say the first tool of recruitment was the empowerment arriving with the notion of being *chosen*. I once asked her how this was different from the narrative of Jesus. She'd smiled. She'd said, "It's not."

I understand One was planting seeds in my mind that summer afternoon. I'm not an idiot. I even understood this at the time. But he was right; I *did* want something more. I *did* see the hypocrisy and futility of everything around me. I kept seeing the bald woman holding the bald man, whispering bits of encouragement, love.

Sometimes I think about there being no accidents, just the shirking of wants. If this is true, then my father led me to One's doorstep. Maybe he did this on purpose. Maybe he knew about a group in the mountains who were all sick and trying to recover together. Maybe he knew I'd gravitate toward the burning lantern of empathy and inclusion. Maybe he did it because he knew he was losing the battle of the twenty feet separating my doorjamb and my bed, the battle differentiating the size of his transgressions. Maybe it was an act of love.

Back when I was fifteen, I'd lie in bed, forcing myself to stay awake. I'd wait for the alcohol-weighted steps of my father to ascend the attic steps. I'd wait to hear his methodical breathing. I'd wait for the thirty seconds of his internal battle, his mind screaming to turn around and take a cold shower, to live another day. Then I'd hear the unmistakable unzipping of his fly. Sometimes I'd wait all night and it wouldn't happen, and this felt like an even greater betrayal.

# 4. MOLLY

I wear my navy-blue shirt when I go to Talley's Tatters. I have my hair slicked back and to the side and I think I look handsome. Talley shows up and she's all smiles in a red dress with white polka dots and a lacy bodice. Her hair is longer, darker, a fifties bob, a wig.

"Told you that shirt would look good," she says.

I thank her. She opens the door and disarms the security system. She turns on the lights. We walk behind the purple cash wrap. She pats the stool next to her. I sit. Our knees are close to touching. She opens her computer and asks what I feel like listening to. I tell her whatever.

"What kind of music do you like?"

"Anything is fine."

"I know this. But I'm asking *you*. What do *you* listen to?"

The last album I downloaded had been three years ago, probably rap. I shake my head.

"Here's the deal, Mason Hues. I've offered you a job. Although this place isn't exactly rocket science—oh, all you have to do is type in the style number of the piece into this screen here, and then take their money, that's it—it's still a job. That means you can at least try to talk."

"Okay."

"Sorry, that came across way bitchier than I wanted it to. What I meant to say is don't be nervous. No wrong answers here, okay? Just two people sitting behind a counter pretending to work. Sound good?"

"Sounds good."

"Now, what do you want to listen to?"

"Elvis."

Talley raises one eyebrow. "I like it."

She puts on a live show, something from the early seventies. She looks around the store and sighs. I feel like I'm failing because I'm too quiet. I try to think of something to say and then I chastise myself for feeling nervous and in need of making small talk. The silence becomes a physical mass. Talley adjusts her wig.

She eventually gets up and tells me to follow. We go to the far side of the store. There are two cardboard boxes full of used clothes. She tells me to hang each item, steam it, more for bedbugs than to get the wrinkles out. I nod and Talley stares and then I apologize.

"For what?"

"For being quiet."

"Shut up," Talley says. She smiles, but it's not a real smile because the skin connecting her ear doesn't tighten. "I'll break you out of your shell. Probably sooner rather than later."

I start steaming clothes. I dig through the lives that people no longer want. I think about people getting too fat or too skinny and then about a husband having died and some widow finally, after two years, mustering the strength to box up his things and drop them off.

The hanging bells above the door ring. A guy walks in with tight jeans and an even tighter T-shirt. He navigates the store like he knows it well. He sneaks up behind Talley and pinches her sides and she screams and laughs and then kisses this boy who might be a man. She presses her chest to his, her hands slipping around and tucking themselves into his back pockets.

I feel jealous.

One always said that jealousy could be a useful tool to gauge the level of which Self was running your life.

I pretend not to watch, to avert my eyes from intimacy.

One and I talked about this tendency of mine on multiple occasions. The first time he brought it up was after I'd been in his house for a week. He asked what, specifically, spoke to me loud enough to come find Truth. I felt embarrassed, as I did any time an adult spoke to me. I told him it'd been what he'd said about looking for something else.

One shook his head.

"Thirty-Seven, it's natural to lie. It's what we're conditioned to do. It's a form of survival. But what good does it do?"

"I'm not lying."

"Whenever somebody tells you they aren't lying, they are."

"I don't think I'm lying."

"What made you come here?"

I thought of something smart to say. I started telling him what I thought he wanted to hear—I was sick of the bullshit life of school and popularity; I was in search of something real and authentic—and then One grabbed the back of my head. He pressed his forehead to mine. I worried he was going to kiss me. His skin was greasy.

"What did you see that made you come here?"

"The couple on the couch. They were sick. They were tender."

The edges of his lips curled upward. "There it is." He let go of my head.

"What?"

"The first honest thing you've said since arriving."

"Thank you."

"Why was that so hard?"

"I don't know."

"Yes, you do."

"Because it felt…"

"Words may be imperfect tools for bearing Honesty, but at times, they are all we have."

"I shouldn't have been looking in the window in the first place."

"There are no accidents."

"I guess."

"You were attracted to a showing of intimacy. A selfless act of love not predicated upon sex. Do you know why?"

I shook my head.

"Because it's the rarest thing on this planet. Unconditional love. Love without sex. Love without expectations. Love of helping somebody worse off than yourself."

Talley introduces me to her boyfriend, Derek. We shake hands and then he's back playing grab-ass with Talley and I steam a small, shelled fleece jacket and think about the boy it belonged to, him leaving home, probably first to college, then to some city that paid for his services, his mother cleaning his closet, her holding the jacket, pressing it to her face, lost for a good five minutes in the memory of him in that coat, his boisterous energy taking up every inch of their home, the stillness since his departure, stillness and silence, her marriage nothing without the active duties of parenthood.

Derek leaves and Talley saunters over. Her energy has changed. She's lighter on her feet.

She says, "He's cute, right?"

I shrug.

"Please, you know he's beautiful."

She obviously wants me to agree, so I smile, nod.

"He's in a band."

"Of course he is."

Talley gives an insulted laugh. "What's that supposed to mean?"

"Nothing. He just looked like a guy who's in a band."

"Beautiful?"

"Beautiful."

"They're good. Really good. Kind of like stoner punk, you know? Like soulful early Ramones."

I have no idea what she's talking about. Elvis sings an uninspired version of "Mystery Train."

"They're playing tonight. You should come."

"Tonight isn't—"

"Shut the fuck up. You're coming."

There is no reason I can't go. There's no reason not to do anything. She walks toward me. She kind of moves to the music and then she moves a little bit more. She takes the shirt I'm steaming off the rack and holds it to her chest, her left arm outstretched. She dances around with it in a circle and she looks back at me and I grin because she needs me to. She needs me to approve of Derek. She needs me to approve of her life. She needs me as a project and a father. I can give her these things. I really can.

I meet Talley outside of A Fine Line at a quarter to ten that night. She wears the same red dress, but she's altered it, cut out the middle, dissecting the garment into a skirt and matching crop. Her belly button is confused if it wants to hide or be seen and her stomach has abdominal definition and she smokes a cigarette. She wraps her arm around me. She smells like alcohol and incense.

She pays my cover. The bouncer is a fat, bearded man who stares at me for too long as he marks both of my hands with giant black X's. Most of the people are white and in their mid-twenties. A bar runs the length of one side of the building. A blonde who looks like she doesn't know how not to be a bartender takes our orders. I ask for a Mr. Pibb. Talley giggles. The bartender tells me she could do a Coke with some grenadine and I tell her that sounds good. Talley has her hand on my back. I feel like an accessory. Somebody has body odor and I realize it's Talley and this smell makes me think of love. She introduces me to a group of people. I don't listen to their names because names don't matter. More people crowd around the high-top. I feel badly for wanting Derek's band to fail because that's really about my own selfish fears. Old Cream plays from the speakers.

Talley turns to me. She digs around in her vintage clutch. She looks over both shoulders. She tells me to stick out my hand. I do. She places two capsules and some sort of hard candy in my palm.

It takes me a second to realize they're drugs of some sort.

"What's wrong?" Talley says.

"Nothing. I didn't want anyone to see."

"All the narcs, you mean?"

I nod

She laughs. She leans forward, kind of yelling into my ear that I'm paranoid. I want to tell her that people who've spent thirty months in locked rooms have the right to be paranoid, but I stay silent.

"Take them now. Derek will go on in like ten minutes. Timing will be perfect."

The only drugs I've ever done were with the family. Every full moon, we sat around a campfire. The only people excused were those in the first two weeks of their treatments. We'd sit around with blankets, all of us staring into the fire, our shoulders touching, sometimes holding onto one another. One called it Reprieve. He said it wasn't a shirking of Self because DMT, above all else, forced somebody against Truth. We'd sit there and we'd be silent and then we'd take our tin foil and then One would give us a sign and then we'd light the foil and we'd breathe in smoke, both the chemical-tasting smoke of the DMT and the thick smoke of the fire, and then we would experience Reprieve.

I ask Talley what the pills are.

"Molly. And the candy is an edible."

I've never taken ecstasy and I'm not sure what it will do to me. At CMHIP, they preached the dangers of drugs with people who've experienced psychiatric trauma.

"It's totally safe," Talley says. She puts her arm around my waist. My elbow brushes against her flat belly. She needs me to approve of her life. Her choices. She needs me to have fun.

"I'll help you through. Be at your side the whole time. You'll love it, I swear."

I glance down at Talley. Her nose is dotted with blackheads. I love this about her.

She says, "After all, I gave you a job…"

"You're going to hold that over my head forever, aren't you?"

"Until you realize the job sucks and quit, yes."

I laugh.

Talley slips two pills into her mouth.

I've ingested worse things.

I swallow the pills and then eat the cherry candy.

We stand and stare at an empty stage. Talley bounces around from person to person. She comes back ten minutes later. She stands on her tiptoes and presses her mouth to my ear. I'd done the same to One my first night in Marble. I'd told him my first love, my favorite memory, and my biggest regret.

Talley says, "What about him?" She points across the bar. A skinny kid dressed in black stands next to a speaker. "I could totally see you together. Hot. It'd be a hot sight."

Talley thinks I'm gay.

I guess this makes sense. It's why she'd kept asking if I thought Derek was cute. It's why she feels okay hanging all over me. It's probably why she gave me a job at her shop. I'm about to correct her, when I stop myself, because it doesn't matter. I am there to serve Tally and to give her what she needs from life because I have nothing and no one and everyone presents false Selves anyway.

"Too skinny," I say.

"Really? Are you a chubby chaser?"

"A what?"

"A chubby chaser. You cruise for brutes?"

"I'm picky."

"Top or bottom?"

I'd been both in juvie. It wasn't rape and it wasn't even true homosexuality. It was the need for intimacy inside of a system designed to alienate the already alienated. The sex had lasted for five days. My cellmate, Jerome, said if I told anyone he'd slit my throat. He ended up smashing my head against the wall three times on the sixth night. Evidently, he believed a preemptive strike was the best course of action. He told everyone I'd tried to touch his junk and then I was simply referred to as *Faggot* and then I quit talking and then I was transferred to CMHIP.

The truth is, I can be anyone Talley wants me to be. I can be any person anyone could ever want.

The band walks out of a side door and onto the stage raised two feet off the floor. Talley screams. Some people clap. Derek has a red guitar around his neck. I wonder if this is why Talley wore the red dress. Derek steps front and center. He thanks us for coming out. He calls us a bunch of cocksuckers. People like this. Sometimes people like to be insulted because it's a form of validation of how they really see themselves. One didn't say that, but it's something he might have thought.

The music starts.

It's too loud, all symbols and mumbled vocals. Talley dances with her hands raised, her head shaking back and forth, the synthetic edges of her hair brushing her chin. The song ends and then they play one that sounds the same. I know I'll have a headache. The third song is a little different, the tempo slower, the drums muted. Derek sings. I listen to his words, something about love and true love and eternal love, and I look over at Talley and she beams the smile of a cherished little girl and then I yawn a big yawn that might have lasted an hour and then everything is amazing. The music no longer is too loud. I want it louder. I want it to fill my capillaries. I want to be touched. I want to be surrounded by more pressing bodies. I want to be given a sponge bath. I want to confess all of these wants and I want to not chastise myself for having desires.

I turn to Talley. She takes one look at me and giggles and then wraps her arms around me. My forehead is so close to pressing against hers.

"How you doing there, Mr. Hues?"

"I feel beautiful."

"You are."

We dance for a long while and my mind's occupied with all the usual suspects of shame and sex and love, but there are new ones tossed in—seeing beauty for the first time in three years, believing myself capable of being something besides a sharer of secrets, the notion of friends who at least liked me—and I try the coping mechanisms they preached in CMHIP, the concentration on a particular color. Yellow, everything is yellow, lens flares and levity and new beginnings, the counting of my shallow breaths—*in, two, three, four, out, two three, four*—the repetition of a single word, love, love, love, and maybe this isn't the best choice because I'm back sitting around a campfire being held by Five and she's telling me I'm the strongest person she knows and beautiful and capable of greatness.

# 5. A LOOSE AND BROAD NARRATIVE

Talley says I'm the little brother she never had. She says she feels more comfortable around me than any other person in her life. She pauses. "Well, maybe not more than Derek."

I smile because this is a correction of formality rather than Truth.

We sit against the brick wall outside of A Fine Line. Derek's band is on set break. I'm destroyed in a good way. I wonder why people don't take drugs all of the time and then I realize they do and they're addicts and they die. This is their own form of chemotherapy. My teeth chatter from deluges of dopamine. Talley has my hand in her lap. She strokes my fingers without noticing.

"You dance so pretty," Talley says.

"You do."

"I feel like you were sent to me."

"Sent how?"

"From the universe or God or something," Talley says.

"There's no God."

"But there's energy."

"Which can neither be created nor destroyed," I say.

"Exactly. That's what I'm saying. My life was lacking something, and you came. It was lacking your exact energy and then you walked through with your cute little bag of applications."

"I got a haircut that day."

"Sexy as fuck."

"Creation myths."

"Fuck Creationists."

"Your dress has a rip in it."

"Do you like?"

"Yeah."

"Do you think I'm going to get married to Derek?"

"No."

"Why?"

"Because sickness bears Honesty and Honesty bears change."

"You think he's not being honest with me?"

"Nobody is honest with anybody."

"I'm honest with you."

"No, you're not."

"I swear to fucking God I have been. What haven't I been honest with you about?"

"It doesn't matter," I say.

"No, serious, what have I lied to you about?"

"To yourself," I say.

Talley quits stroking my hand. She shivers against me or maybe that's me shivering against her.

"Ask me anything, and I'll tell you the truth," Talley says.

"That's impossible."

"No, it's not. Like the CIA or some shit used Molly like truth serum. Impossible to lie on this stuff."

"Who was the first person you loved?"

"Jared Boykin."

I laugh at the last name. Talley hits me and then takes hold of my hand and brings my entire arm to her lap. She wraps her bent knees around my elbow.

"What about him did you love?"

"He was the sexiest guy in the tenth grade."

"How did it end?"

"Missy Bowman blew him at a party my parents wouldn't let me go to."

I nod. Talley turns. She says, "See, hundred percent honesty."

I shake my head, but I'm too high to press the subject. She tells me it's my turn.

"I've never been in love," I say.

"Bullshit."

"Not love like that."

"Then tell me something True. Anything."

"I've done bad things."

"We've all done bad things."

"I am steeped in want."

"We're all *steeped in want*."

"I know more about people than probably ninety-nine percent of the population."

"Besides how to interact with them."

"None of what I'm saying is true. It's true, but not really. It's true, but it's also warped with how I want you to view me."

"How do you want me to view you?"

"I don't know."

"You want to know how I see you?"

I nod.

"You're sweet. You're scared. You're confused. You're in need of something deeper than all this bullshit."

"A loose and broad narrative."

"How do you see me?"

"Beautiful and broken and trying really hard."

"Ouch," Talley says.

"That was close to Honesty."

"Do you think Derek cheats on me?"

"Yes."

Talley quits smiling. The thought of Derek loving another girl is evidently enough to puncture her chemical euphoria. She starts crying or maybe she's simply sniffling from the sudden drop in temperature.

We're quiet.

A girl in a miniskirt yells into her cellphone. A couple walks their husky mutt. A cab creeps by and the driver's skin is invisible in the black night.

"Why do guys cheat?"

"Because they are scared of dying."

"That's a bullshit response."

"It doesn't matter."

"What do they want?"

"To break time through love."

"You're a poet."

"I'm an actor."

"Is this conversation Honest?"

"Closer than most."

"Why don't you exist online?"

"I don't have a computer," I say.

"That's not the real reason."

"But it's *a* reason."

"Who are you really?"

"Thirty-Seven."

"Thirty-seven what?"

"Minutes we've been out here."

"We should go in."

"Okay."

"Do you like the music?"

"It's growing on me."

"You never answered my question before. About your first love. Who's the guy who broke that cute little heart of yours for the first time?"

I stand. It's freezing not pressed against Talley. She extends her hands. I take them and drape her arms around my neck.

"I've never been in love," I say.

"Right, that's what you say. Then tell me something else. Something *true*, as you keep calling it."

"Sometimes Truth is equivalent to want."

"Then what do you want? Right this minute. What do you want to do more than anything?"

I speak with as much Honesty as I can. "To press my forehead against yours."

Talley doesn't laugh. She doesn't even smile. She stands on her tiptoes and leans forward and then she presses forward and I close my eyes and press back, and we push harder, push and push, sweat and grease and pressure, and I breathe in her body odor and feel lust and communion, and it's One pushing back, One inviting me into his family and into his soul, One demonstrating we are equals because we are riddled with flaws. I open my eyes. Talley has hers open, too, like she knows that the whites of the eyes can't lie.

# 6. SELF TO OTHER

I was scared when I arrived at One's house. I was scared because I'd run away and because nobody went by actual names, just numbers, and because the whole scene struck me as rather cultish. But mostly, I was scared because everyone was sick.

I'd never been around sick people. I had a friend whose younger brother died of cancer but that whole experience was kept at the sterile distance of *get well* cards and an uncomfortable suit standing in a cemetery in the autumn of my tenth year on this earth. I was scared of germs. I hated the flu. I didn't even like being around old people, their bodies in the throes of rapid decay.

Then why did I show up with only a backpack at One's door?[3]

Everyone was thin. So thin. The kind of thin that anorexia only made a feeble mockery of. Their eyes—Five's and Twenty-Six's and even One's—were set so deep within their ashen tombs. The black scrubs hung off of their frames. Elbows were the prominent feature. Bald heads. Stained teeth. Constant looks of exhaustion. Inhales with a wince; exhales with an excruciating closing of the eyes.

---

3 Dr. Turner kept asking why I joined The Survivors until I told her about my father. Then she changed her question: "What catalyzing event occurred the night you ran away?"

One had his arm around my shoulder. He brought me through the main room with its couches and pillows and lounging sick. The ceiling was two stories high, three in the front. They tried to smile. They tried to hug me. They tried to tell me I was brave. The overwhelming smell was a lemony cleaner. I looked inside of paint buckets filled with bright yellow bile. *Welcome, Thirty-Seven.* I told myself it was better than home. I told myself these people weren't contagious. I told myself I'd been led here by my father.

The kitchen was beautiful, cedar logs and a marble island and stainless-steel appliances. One opened the refrigerator. There were rows and rows of grape Pedialyte. One brought me down a hallway. The walls were bare, but I saw the sun-stained outline of once-hung pictures. He opened a door to a bedroom with four sets of bunk beds. Bald people slept. The smell wasn't citrus cleaner, but vomit. He showed me another room with more of the same. And then two more. One told me everyone moved a single bed upwards a day. This was to ensure none of us got too comfortable with the material, while also fostering a larger *circle of trust.*

One brought me downstairs. The basement was finished and pretty with its logs and lush carpet. People lay around on pillows. A woman held a feather to a man's face. She traced his closed eyes. He tried to smile or maybe tried not to.

I needed to leave.

This—whatever it was—wasn't for me. I wasn't a hippie and I didn't believe in God and I wasn't sick and didn't want that to change. I was a kid. I was the youngest person by at least five years.

"You're looking a little pale, Thirty-Seven," One said.

"I'm fine."

"Let's grab some fresh air."

"Okay."

I followed One up the stairs. I'd get outside and then leave. I'd tell him I'd made a mistake. I'd tell him I was sorry for wasting his time.

We walked out the patio door. The mountains were big and black. I was finally able to breathe. One led me down some wooden stairs. We took a path that started out cobblestone but turned into dirt after a few minutes. I thought about running. One's breathing was labored from the slight incline. I felt like Hansel.

We reached a small outcropping of rocks. One climbed halfway up, then reached his hand back. I didn't want to touch him but I put my arm out anyway. We climbed on top of a boulder. We stood there overlooking the house and the river, a view I knew he'd paid millions for.

"Sit, sit," One said.

I sat. The granite dug into my skin through my jeans. One sat next to me. He didn't say anything. Men never said anything in my presence; their silence was the sound of sins being committed.

"I come out here to think," One said.

I nodded, waiting for him to continue. He didn't, at least not for a long while. A woodpecker with a red back hammered its beak into a dead pine.

"You have acted on the faith that our family here has something to offer you. Something you are not receiving at home. I'm sure you have questions; this is only natural. I will do everything in my power to answer your questions as Honestly as I can."

He looked at me. I pretended to be looking at the woodpecker, but was really just trying to avoid eye contact.

"What are they sick with?"

"We are sick with selfishness forced upon us by a society that cares nothing for a single one of us. However, if you are asking the cause of our portrayed physical symptoms, the answer is Cytoxan, a nitrogen mustard alkylating agent used to treat various forms of cancer, as well as select autoimmune diseases."

I didn't say anything.

"A form of chemotherapy."

"Because they have cancer?"

"Because sickness bears Honesty."

"So there's…"

"Physically speaking, *no*, there is nothing wrong with us. We are voluntarily undergoing chemotherapy. We are breaking down our physical, emotional, and spiritual selves in order to free ourselves from the shackles of everything we know. We are rebuilding ourselves among a loving family of our own choosing. We are trusting people who have experienced the same struggles. We are building Honesty. We are creating Truth."

I nodded. I had kind of quit listening. I needed to get away from this guy and from the rest of these freaks. I stretched my back, hoping it signified my intention to leave.

"But what is it you really want to know?" One said. "What aren't you asking?"

I shook my head. I pretended to be struck with a thought. I said, "Can't you die from this?"

"That's a risk we are all willing to take."

"Where did everyone come from?"

"Families of origin do not matter."

"Oh."

"Take, for instance, your own. Your father, whom you were out fishing with the other month."

I could feel One's stare.

"I know he's done things," One said.

I glanced to my left. One's face was a carving etched in golden Basswood.

"My father—we don't talk about our previous selves here, except, of course, when we're introducing a new family member to
our way of life—was a sick man. Alcoholic. Abusive, in every way
imaginable. We grew up dirt poor because he couldn't keep a job.
When I was eleven years old, I watched him strike my older sister
with a wrench. She fell, hitting her temple on the corner of the
table. She died three days later in the hospital."[4]

One paused. He took off his wool beanie. There wasn't even the
hint of stubble on his bald head.

"So I know what it's like to need to leave. I know what it feels
like to have an ideal of family in your head juxtaposed to your
*actual* family."

I was about to tell him that my father had never touched me.
The words gurgled in my throat. I coughed.

"I know what it's like to keep secrets. I know what it's like to
feel responsible for hateful actions. *It was my fault my sister died
because I'd somehow made my father mad, he only touched me because I had been stupid to walk around the house in my underwear.*
This list is endless. All of it misguided attempts to gain control over
the uncontrollable. All of it selfish. Counselors and shrinks will
tell us the same thing. They'll say it wasn't our faults, our abus-
ers were sick people, we are victims, which is true, but does us no
good. Why? Because there is nothing more comfortable than the
role of victim."

---

4 Dr. Turner snuck in Henry O'Connor's *Dr. Sick: The Survivors and The
Day of Gifts*, and allowed me to read it. She said it would help "dethrone"
Dr. James Shepard once I learned the truth about his actual life. I read
all five hundred pages in a day. I believed most of it. In the second chapter, after the sensationalized semifictional opening of how O'Connor
envisioned the murders, it stated that James Shepard grew up as a single
child on Fifth Avenue in New York City, his father a leading hedge fund
manager at Goldman, his mother a socialite, a cousin through marriage
to the Rockefellers.

I nodded.

"And once we really embrace that role, entrenching ourselves as hapless bystanders to others' abuse, we will seek it out in every relationship we ever have. We will manifest this same dynamic. We will pass it to our children. We will bear victimization."

The sun had set but the sky was still light, or at least not dark.

"What we are doing here is changing all of that. This isn't bullshit psychotherapy or some crackpot religion, this is fundamentally changing the people we are. Scientifically, we are different people after chemotherapy. Emotionally different. Spiritually different. There is no way to be brought to the brink of death through the destruction of ourselves, only to be nursed back to health through a loving family of *our own choosing*, and not be a different person. A person who, above all else, leads with Honesty."

I was scared.

I was scared because I didn't want to experience pain and because these people were completely crazy and because I didn't want to return home and because some of what he said made sense.

"We are free to leave at any point. We are free to do whatever we want. But most of all, we are free of our pasts."

I was fifteen.

I was fifteen and scared.

I was fifteen and they called me Thirty-Seven.

I was fifteen, unsure of anything, entitled to the notion of happiness and love, terrified I'd done something to elicit my father's masturbation in my doorway, petrified I'd done something to force my birth parents to want no part of me.

"This is the most heroic journey a person can ever take," One said.

"What?"

"The journey from Self to Other."

I wasn't sure what this meant but I nodded anyway.

"Let's try something," One said. "We know you are scared about being here. We all were. That's natural."

"Okay."

"We want to give you some reprieve from the pain you are in. Does that sound like something you would want?"

"For sure."

"This is a single drop worth of easement compared to the ocean of tranquility you will eventually experience."

I looked up. One smiled. The sky was finally dark behind him; the edges of his face were sharp in contrast.

"I need you to tell me three things. In telling me these three things, I need you to be as Honest as you possibly can. Try your best to leave your answers unfiltered. Reach as deep as your current self will allow for Truth."

"Okay."

One scooted toward me. Our legs touched. He leaned forward and down, pushing the side of his head near my face.

"Speak directly into my ear."

I'd been right about One being some sick bastard and this cult being crazy. He was going to try to blow me. If I'd wanted that, I could have simply stayed home and dropped a hint.

He asked me about my first love. I brought my lips near his ear. I told him. He asked me what my favorite memory was. I closed my eyes and tried to be Honest and I didn't recoil when my lips grazed the soft blond hairs lining his ear. And then he asked me my biggest regret and my lips were pressed firmly to his ear, my tongue making contact with his cavern on certain stressed consonants, and something was happening, something I couldn't explain, something inside of me, something with lightness, something with colors bursting across my closed eyelids, something with warmth and pleasure and being one hundred percent grounded in the moment—the slightly painful granite, the earthy tang of pine, the crispness of sudden shade—and I felt something wet against my lips and thought it was coming from One's ear, but soon I realized it was mine—my tears, my tears as I told another man the three largest forces keeping me in everlasting servitude to a broken worldview of Self.

One turned to me.

He cried as well.

He reached behind my head and pressed his forehead to mine. We kept our eyes open. My body was a thousand versions of postcoital humming. He didn't have to tell me he was proud. That I'd done well, that on some fundamental level, he loved me. And likewise, I didn't have to tell him I would stay, that I'd been searching for this my entire life. That I was ready to take this process to the next level, my fear of needles and sickness nothing in comparison to the intoxicating feelings of inclusion and vulnerability and love.

# 7. CYTOXAN

We had to wait two weeks before we started our treatments. I protested and said I was ready and everyone shook their heads, told me this was a decision not to be taken lightly. They said it was wise to be around the suffering. They said it was important to read the literature of what Cytoxan could do. But they told me this in a kind way with brotherly and sisterly concern. I felt left out but not excluded.

I read that Cytoxan could cause infertility. That it could lead to acute myeloid leukemia. Hemorrhagic cysts. Bladder cancer. I read about lowered white blood cell counts and infections that could take lives. Hair loss. Vomiting. Diarrhea. Fatigue.

I helped as much as I could.

I helped with the laundry. I helped with vacuuming. I helped scrubbing vomit-crusted buckets. I helped by being there and being healthy and having energy.

I watched IV drips being administered. One had been a doctor, an oncologist in his previous life. That was how he knew what to do and that was how he had money for the amazing house and that was probably why he'd decided on chemo as a tool for bearing Honesty in the first place. He'd been around it; he'd administered

IV bags full of poison to people who knew they were going to die. He'd seen the benefits of a complete stripping of Self.

I gave a sponge bath to Five, a woman of thirty who made me think of alien abductions. She was attractive in a strange way or maybe it was just her voice, so soft, everything a whispered secret. We sat on the floor of the smallest bedroom. It was just her and I. She removed her clothes and I felt bashful and she told me not to be embarrassed. I apologized. She told me not to apologize. I ran a loofah over her shoulders. Her clavicles were entrenched foxholes. Her nipples hardened underneath my sponging. The only hair she had on her body was underneath her arms. She told me it was okay to look. I nodded. She told me it was okay to have feelings of lust; it was dishonest to pretend they weren't there.

I would go on walks in the afternoon. Sometimes I would go with the others. With them, I'd walk slowly. I'd offer my support over rocks. I'd tell them they were doing really well. When it was just me, I'd go quickly. I'd work up a sweat and sometimes I ran and I wasn't sure why—I wasn't a huge fan of any sort of physical activity—but it felt right. I'd work up a sweat, my pulse thundering in my ears, my legs going numb, and then I'd finally stop. I'd look out over the mountains that were now my home. I'd pretend I was suffering an attack of symptoms. I'd imagine myself sick. I'd envision myself getting better.

My time with One became sacred. It was like he was everywhere at once. He seemed to understand exactly who needed him the most. I'd round the corner, and somebody I knew was close to giving up would be crying in his arms. Time after time, he sought out the ones in need. He had his fingers to the pulse of the entire family. And when my mind started to stray, thoughts about this being so crazy gaining momentum, he'd find me. He'd ask me to take a walk. We'd go to our boulder. I'd tell him my fears. We would put our foreheads together. He'd tell me I was doing well. That he was proud.

Two weeks came and went and I was still there in the mountains of Marble. People smiled when I walked into rooms. I felt useful. I learned how to fold hospital corners. I knew Cytoxan was a carcinogen. I knew there was more than a slight chance of the drug causing my death. I'd held a knife above my wrist two weeks before, forty-nine to fifty-one percent suicide or running away. The hypothetical pain seemed like a treat; everything was theoretical. One asked if I'd made a decision. I told him I had.

That night, the thirty-seven of us gathered around a fire. I knew how hard this was for certain people in the midst of agony, but they did it, not complaining, that pinch of a pain-racked smile. I was nervous, but more excited. People congratulated me. People rubbed my back. People kissed my cheek.

One stood up. We all watched. The flames illuminated half of his face. He didn't wear his beanie. Half of his head shone. He talked about this being the most special of nights. He said it was the most heroic action a young man could take. He said the universe bringing me to their door was proof that their way of life was gaining momentum. He looked at me. I had to fight back a smile. He said, "Thirty-Seven is poised for greatness. The capacity for Honesty in him is as immense as I've ever seen. Inversely, so too is his capacity for deceit. It is our job as his loving family of his own choosing to guide him in this transition. We must be diligent in feeding only his wolf of Honesty."

I nodded. One stared. I wondered if I was supposed to do something.

Finally, One said, "Thirty Seven, I speak for all of us when I say that we love you more than we love ourselves."

People clapped.

I smiled.

He motioned for me to stand.

I did. We stood next to the fire, encircled by thirty-five others. He took my head in his hand and pressed his forehead to mine and I loved the whites of his eyes. He said, "Are you ready to destroy yourself?"

"Yes."

"Are you ready to change the world?"

"Yes."

He let go. I felt pressure against my back. Five stood there. Her eyebrow ridges were smooth. She walked in front of me. She unzipped my sweatshirt. She guided my arms out of the sleeves. She took the bottom of my T-shirt and pulled it upward. I felt like a little boy being undressed. I wasn't sure what was happening. She undid my belt. She unzipped my fly. I thought of my father. She helped me out of my pants. She wrapped her fingers under the elastic of my boxers and I felt nervous and slightly excited and then I was naked and I was embarrassed because I had an erection but nobody laughed.

She took hold of my left arm. She turned it so my wrist faced the sky. Her hands trembled against my skin. I knew she was tired and sick and maybe this wasn't a good idea and I was so scared. One approached me with a needle. It was my turn to shake. He wiped the crook of my elbow with an alcohol swab. He didn't wear gloves. I watched a needle go into my skin. He slipped a different device into my arm. He held a drip bag of some sort. Five took it, holding it above her shoulders. The tube was connected. Everyone stood and clapped and the fire crackled and I wasn't cold anymore. I felt sickness enter my body. I still had an erection. Everyone was so happy for me. I was happy for me or maybe I was simply happy.

# 8. SICK (I)

The violence with which I vomited at three the next morning burst a blood vessel in my left eye. It was completely red, not a sliver of white. There was nothing inside of me; there was always more to come out. I cried. Somebody rubbed my back. My body expelled poison. Again and again and again. The reprieve between vomits was less than a minute long. The grape Pedialyte was the worst taste I'd ever ingested. My body forced the lining of my stomach out of my mouth. I cried even harder.

# 9. OPTIONS

I don't worry about money. At least not really, not like the rest of the world. There are several reasons. First, I was given a "transition settlement" by the government. This was decided upon when I became anonymous in exchange for my testimony. It's not much—food stamps, medical insurance, two years' rent in Section 8 housing—but it provides the basics. I simply have to meet with a probation officer once a month, stay out of trouble, and remain anonymous in regards to The Survivors.

The second reason I don't worry about money is because I don't want for much. Sure, I'm a human in the world and am slowly growing the material covets of the masses, but certain beliefs have attached themselves to my most primal strands of DNA. One always said money was not the root of people's problems; it was the misguided belief system that happiness came through addition rather than subtraction.

Thirdly, if I ever find myself in a desperate situation, or if I somehow experience a radical mental rearrangement, I could become a multimillionaire overnight. How? Break my anonymity. Agree to interviews. Sell my soul to one of the major studios. I don't see this ever being a viable option, but it's exactly that, an option.

I once read something about options having a negative effect on people's happiness. I believe this. It probably correlates with what One said about subtraction rather than addition. But the article also said something about *not* having options. If a person does not have a single option—this in itself is a falsity, because there are always options—then he experiences an even greater amount of unhappiness. I guess this makes sense too.

Sometimes my life seems like nothing but options. I have nowhere to really be and no one to be accountable to. I could do anything. This thought often fills me with dread. Sometimes I long for structure. Sometimes I wish an underpaid guard would bang on my metal door and tell me to wake the fuck up. Sometimes I wish I knew the first half of my week would be occupied with vomiting and cramps so severe I prayed for death, then two days of fatigue, then two days of dread awaiting my next treatment.

I bring this up to Talley. It's two days after we'd gone to see Derek's band. We're at work. She's training me on how to close the store. The day has been good and our conversation jocular and I feel like our rolling has strengthened our relationship instead of made it weird. Talley complains about having nothing to do that night. She says Derek's practicing with his band. She tells me it might be fun to head over there and listen. Then she says she just kind of wants to get a drink and go home.

What she's *not* saying is *I want Derek to leave band practice and come over and spoon me on the couch*, but this want is obvious.

"What are you up to?" she says.

"Nothing much."

"*Nothing much.* What is it that you do when you're not here?"

"Read."

"I'll take that as a whole lot of dick pic Snapchatting."

We laugh.

"Eat. Climb into bed. Read. Sleep."

"Sounds like a convict's life," Talley says.

I've honestly never thought about this fact, but yes, it is.

"Where do you live?" she asks.

"Mile away."

"In your parents' basement?"

"Thankfully, no."

"Bullshit," Talley says. "It makes so much sense. How did I never see it before? Weird Loner Boy lives at home. Eating your mom's casserole—"

"Sounds rather Oedipal."

"What? Gross."

"Your words."

"Watching their premium cable before retiring to your room still decorated in Star Wars figurines."

"My parents are dead."

Talley's face flattens. She stares at me for a second before I drop my gaze. I'm not sure why I lied. I mean, it's technically a lie, but functionally true. My parents have been dead to me for three years. They've been dead to me years before that. Talley is at my side. She touches my arm, and seeing I'm receptive to her physical contact, she embraces me. I know why I lie. Everyone knows why he lies. I think about being locked up and how the only thing I wanted, even above my freedom, was to be held. To be touched. To be validated as a physical specimen.

"I'm sorry. I'm such a bitch. I didn't—"

"It's fine."

"No, really, I'm sorry. Okay? I feel horrible."

One always said that apologies were inherently selfish because they were thinly veiled cries for pardon, validation, and esteem-building on the behalf of the one amending.

"I never would've said anything…"

"You didn't know."

"I'm sorry."

"It's all good," I say. I try to smile. Talley mirrors my efforts.

"How'd they…"

"Cancer."

"Fuck. Both of them?"

"My mom. My dad…" I look out across the store. I feel like crying and like an actor and like I'm telling an emotional Truth. "He took his life."

"Fuck me," Talley says

"Good times," I say.

Talley frowns. She has her fingers clasped through the front belt loops of my jeans. She says, "You don't have to do that."

"What?"

"Pretend it doesn't hurt."

Talley insists on walking me home. I suppose she feels bad for bringing up my parents, whom I've theoretically killed in order to gain sympathy. She walks with her arm through mine. She lights a cigarette and is careful to blow the smoke away from my face. A homeless man with legs stopping at his kneecaps begs for money. I point to the brick building behind him.

"This is you?" Talley says.

"This is me."

"It's cute."

"It's a shithole."

"Aren't you going to invite me up?"

"I don't have…it's kind of embarrassing."

"Please, I grew up with two brothers. I could care less about your semen-crusted socks. We'll hang out. Order food. Watch TV."

"I don't have TV."

"Right, you *read*. Then we'll do that. I'm not taking no for an answer."

I roll my eyes like I'm put out, but really I'm happy. We walk into the hallway. TVs blare through thin sheetrock. I lead her into the stairwell and she makes a comment about this being exactly the type of staircase women get raped in. We climb four sets. The temperature rises a good five degrees. The Vietnamese family at the end of the hall fills the muggy air with the smell of their cooking. I pause when I'm unlocking my door.

"Don't laugh."

"I'm not a bitch, Mason."

"And don't give that pitying frown either."

She hits my chest. I open the door and step into the apartment. It feels different with her presence. What has been more than adequate suddenly feels pathetic. The walls are white, the cabinets, too. A twin mattress lies on the floor in the far corner. The sheets are immaculately made. The wooden floor is scratched, but it's spotless, shining from my every-other-day waxing by hand.

I turn around. Talley nods her head like she's impressed. She says it's cute.

"The worst liar I've ever met," I say.

"No, I'm being for real. Sparse, clean lines. I like it."

"Do you remember nothing of our conversation about Honesty?"

Talley laughs. "Not really. Only that you kept telling me Derek was going to cheat."

"I didn't say that."

"Did."

"I don't think so."

"You can lie to yourself, but you can't lie to me," Talley says. She pokes me in the ribs and walks the fifteen feet of my studio and sits down on the bed. She starts unclasping her shin-high boots.

"Do your feet stink?"

Talley looks insulted. "Oh my God, quit being such a..."

"Queer?"

"Pussy."

"Pretty sure straight people can have aversions to people's stinky feet all over their beds."

"What, like this?" Talley peels off her socks, then lies back on my mattress, pushing her feet flat against the sheets, gliding them up and down. She laughs and I do too. I walk across the apartment and grab her knees and playfully push her legs off my bed. I sit down in their place.

"Here," Talley says. "Smell them. Like lavender on high noon on the Fourth of July."

"Get those barking dogs out of my face."

Talley waves her feet around my head and I'm laughing, trying to cover my nose as she presses her toes against my cheeks. I pretend to gag and we laugh and then her legs are in my lap, my arms over her shins.

"Do you like have a maid or something?"

"No, why?"

"This place is spotless. There's not a single speck of dirt or dust or anything."

"That's what happens when you have no TV or computer."

"Very Spartan living. Very *strange* living."

"I'm kind of strange."

"Understatement of the century," Talley says.

"At least my feet don't stink."

"Stop. Do they really smell?"

I shrug. Talley brings her foot to her nose and tells me I'm a liar and then puts her legs back over mine. She tells me I'm going to give her a complex.

"My gift to you."

"Speaking of gifts, being in this den of luxury sparks a few ideas."

"I don't need anything."

"Nobody needs anything," Talley says. "But that doesn't mean I can't give you a present or two."

"No, because I don't have the money to get you anything right now," I say.

"You're missing the point of a present," Talley says.

"Don't."

"You, Mr. Mason Hues, are not the boss of me."

"Are you five years old?"

"Maybe," Talley says. She inches her bare feet back toward my face. We're kids laughing. I cup her foot. I feel her pulse along its arch. She tells me to never stop whatever I'm doing. I press with two fingers, slowly working in a clockwise circle around her pressure point. Five taught me this. She said it relieved nausea. She said you could do it to yourself, but it wasn't the same because it lacked the energy of love.

Talley puts her hands behind her head. She moans. I try to keep my thoughts platonic. Five had told me it was okay to become aroused. But I'd been a different person then—younger, immature, quicker to equate attention and physical contact with sex.

Talley has quit with her fake moaning. She holds a thick black book. My body immediately seizes, even my fingers massaging Talley's pressure point. She says *ouch*. She looks over the cover of *Dr. Sick: The Survivors and The Day of Gifts*.

"So this is the light, breezy bedtime reading you were talking about."

I don't know what to say. I need her to not open the book, not to see the copious notes I've taken over the course of its twenty-plus readings. But I can't just grab it. I can't tell her to put it down. I can't draw more attention to its presence.

"I think I should wash my hands after touching these things," I say.

"Dick."

"What do you want to do?"

Talley doesn't answer. She turns the book around. She stares at what I know is a black-and-white photograph of Dr. James Shepard.

"This dude's creepy as fuck."

"Should we order food?"

"Like Manson on steroids."

"Chinese?"

"Can you imagine how fucked up you'd have to be to join this dude? Be like *sure, I'd love to put myself through chemo and then slaughter a bunch of people*? Like who does that?"

"People with no other options."

Talley sets the book down at the foot of my mattress. She says, "I guess. But *still*?"

"Crazy."

"Batshit crazy. I mean, chemo is supposed to be like the most mis…fuck, Jesus Christ, I did it again. I'm sorry."

It takes a split second to remember my alleged, cancer-devoured mother.

I say, "At least you've proven that you're flexible enough to put your foot in your mouth."

Talley laughs. She sits up. She rests her head on my shoulder. She puts her arm around my neck. She pulls me down next to her.

She positions me so I face the wall. She slips her arm underneath my head and then wraps her left arm around my stomach.

"You strike me as the little spoon type," she says.

"Fact," I say.

"Why does it feel so good?"

"What?"

"To be held?"

"Because love is the only thing that stops our march toward death."

"You're kind of a dark motherfucker, aren't you?"

We laugh because it's True and her breasts rise and fall against my back.

"Maybe you should mellow out on the reading and get a TV. Watch some trashy reality shows. See the world for what it actually is."

"And what's that?"

"A complete clusterfuck. But a comical one."

"I like that," I say.

"Yeah?"

"Yeah."

"That makes me happy," she says.

"That I like what you said?"

"Yeah, sort of. Like I had a thought deep enough for Captain Death McHonesty."

"Sorry we all can't be Sexy Whimsical Girl."

"You'd be a pretty girl."

"I know."

"You think I'd be a handsome boy?"

"Thought you were a boy when I saw you without your wig."

Talley play-pinches my nipple. "I would totally fuck you if I had a dick."

"And I would totally let you."

"Yeah? That's the sweetest thing you've ever said," Talley says. She laughs into my ear.

"Sweeter than saying I liked your previous comment?"

"Tied."

"That's fair."

We are quiet. Talley nestles her nose in the nook of my neck. Things are prefect and things are rooted in falsity and every single one of my actions is a manifestation of selfish want.

"You know what the weird thing is?" Talley says.

"Huh?"

"All I wanted to do tonight was spoon with Derek and talk."

"I know," I say.

"How?"

"Because I know how people work."

"Okay, Dr. Freud."

"Fine, don't believe me."

"Then what am I thinking right now?"

I tell her I'm not a psychic. She says, "Exactly my point. You don't know shit. Can't claim superhero powers if you can't even tell me what I'm thinking at this exact moment."

But I *do* know.

I know she's processing this experience through the machine of Self, my lifelike change through an old-fashioned sorter, my existence—past, present, future—only existing as an extension of Talley's visions of her own future. I know she is thinking about my sexuality. She's wondering if I'm sure, if I'm committed to a lifetime of men, if I've ever been with a girl. I know she's mad at herself for wondering these things. I know she's putting on the guilt of infidelity to see how it feels, if it's something she could cope with. Now she's thinking about Derek and his band and the small space they rent to practice and she's thinking about the drugs they're doing and the other bands hanging out in decrepit hallways and a girl, a rhythm guitarist who practices next door, who, more than likely, has made numerous drunken passes at Derek. Talley suddenly knows Derek has kissed this girl. Kissed her with tongue, maybe even flexed his hips against hers before stopping, telling her he has a girlfriend. I know that Talley knows this kiss didn't stop there. But she won't allow herself to go any further. She hates herself for this tendency, a replica of her mother's willful ignorance at her husband's late nights at the office.

I know all of this—not because I can read minds—but because humans are all fundamentally the same. We are a desk of control switches in a recording studio. Our only differences are the volume levels and mixing effects. Our desires are the beating drums. Our choruses are the unshakable beliefs of our selves. The opening stanzas are our first loves. The second stanzas are our favorite memories. The bridges are an ode to our fears. The final stanzas are our biggest regrets.

It's sex, happiness, and the fear of not being able to atone for our wrongs.

But I don't say these things. Instead, I say, "You're thinking that you want to order Chinese food?"

Talley laughs. "Not quite, but I'm straight up starving."

# 10. SICK (II)

The ache in my teeth was unbearable. It felt as if the insides of each tooth—the deep center of my molars, the thin inners of my canines—had been infused with sugar and hydrochloric acid. Every breath caused a spiking of pain. Drinking anything was paper cuts over exposed nerve endings. I asked for medicine, anything, Tylenol or Advil, just please give me something. My tongue felt swollen. Words were too hard to push past my dying teeth.

# 11. GIFTS

Talley buys me a laptop. She says she had it lying around, but it's new. I tell her I can't take it and she tells me to shut up. She pecks my lips. She gives me her Netflix account information so I can watch movies or shows. She gives me my first paycheck and it's more than I should've gotten and I feel like a charity case and like I have a friend.

Life begins to get easier.

She increases my hours so I'm working four shifts a week. I know she doesn't need me at the store, but I can also tell she likes my company.

Sometimes women need a project. Sometimes women need to feel listened to. Maybe everyone needs these things.

I meet with my probation officer for the second time. He makes me piss in a cup. I worry it'll be dirty but he doesn't say anything. His name is Thomas Mack. He's black and has those blotches of darkened spotting on his cheeks. He doesn't know who I am. My record is sealed. I'm nothing but an appointment to him. He asks how I'm adjusting. I tell him I'm adjusting just fine. I show him my payment stub from Talley's Tatters. He makes a copy for my file. He asks what I'm doing with my time. I tell him I got a computer and am watching *Lost*. He seems pleased with this. He tells me he's jealous.

"Why?"

"To have years of shitty television to catch up on."

Talley buys me a lamp. It's an antique or maybe just old, chipped white paint, a floral shade, effeminate. I tell her she needs to stop buying me things. She tells me to just say *thanks*.

I eat rice and drink Mr. Pibb.

I sort and hang and steam clothes.

I see Talley's bare chest when she changes in front of me.

I play the role she needs me to play. I listen to the daily ups and downs of a twenty-something's relationship with a guy who wants to be a rock star.

I keep my money in my pillowcase.

I'm not happy, but I'm not unhappy. Maybe that's the most I can ask for.


It's morning, and Talley and I sit at work. She nurses a hangover while I dust the shoe display.

"I know your secret," Talley says.

I spin around. Talley nods her head, her eyebrows raised. "Yup. Your little *deep thoughts with Mason Hues*. Know you're kind of a phony."

"What?"

Talley reaches into her leather purse. She pulls out a paperback version of *Dr. Sick*. She waves it like a piece of damning evidence. My mind is a series of panicked thoughts and there's no way she'd have been able to peg me as Thirty-Seven, but maybe there is, like maybe she's put two and two together—my highlighted copy of *Dr. Sick*, my age, my lack of possessions, my guarded history—and I make sure to keep my jaw relaxed so the skin connecting my ear doesn't tighten.

She opens the book. She says, "And I quote, 'Dr. James Shepard's mantra, if one is able to wade through the multitude of conflicting

platitudes, would be *sickness bears honesty, and honesty bears change.'*
Sound familiar?"

"So?"

"So? Here I thought you were like some boy genius guru
preaching all this shit. But it's straight from the book."

She's not referring to me being Thirty-Seven, only that I'd
gained my wisdom from the book. I smile and shrug. I say, "What
do you expect? It's what I'm reading."

"Poser."

"Maybe."

"But that's okay," Talley says.

"Thanks for your pardon."

"Ooh, did I strike a nerve? Was that a little flashing of your
teeth?"

"No. Yeah. Sorry."

"No, no, it's cool. Kind of sexy."

I turn back to the rows of discarded shoes. I pick up a leather
topsider and dust its inside.

"It's good," Talley says. "The book, I mean."

I nod, still facing the wall.

"I finished it in like two days. There's something about the
whole thing…"

I don't respond.

"Cults, you know? Why is it people have such a fascination
with them?"

"Beats me."

"You know what I think it is?"

I turn. I shake my head.

"It's kind of like how when people say that the real fear of
standing on a cliff isn't that you'll fall, but that you'll jump. You
know what I mean? People are obsessed with cults because it's so

easy to see yourself falling into one. That, I think, is what really draws us to them."

"Or because they killed a bunch of people," I say.

"But that's precisely my point: people can see themselves joining in a group like this, becoming brainwashed, and eventually becoming so delusional that they murder innocent families."

"There's no such thing as brainwashing."

Talley holds up the book again. "I beg to differ."

"Those people showed up at his door. He didn't *recruit* them. They were looking for something."

"They were looking for *anything*. Which this sick fuck provided them with. Which, I'm pretty sure, is the definition of *brainwashing*."

"Maybe," I say.

"Maybe? How is that *maybe*? Any time someone else's thoughts are forced down your throat until they become your own, that's brainwashing."

"But what if our own thoughts are the problem?"

"The problem with *what*?"

"Life."

Talley laughs. She squints her eyes. She tells me I can't be serious. I know this moment can go one of two ways; I can be Honest, or I can lie. I have options. I have choices.

I smile. I say, "Okay, you're right: I'm a fraud. But it doesn't mean I'm any less rad."

Talley and I hang out a few nights a week. It's no coincidence these nights fall on evenings when Derek's band has practice. We make a little routine of picking up food and walking to my apartment. We sit on my bed and talk and touch and eat. It's weird to eat in bed. I fear a guard will burst through my door and write me up. I fear the loss of rec time. We watch movies I've never heard of on my laptop.

Talley has a preference for coming-of-age films with a broken female lead. I can't stop crying during *Girl, Interrupted*. Talley holds me. She strokes my face. One night she sleeps over, which is nice. She snores a little bit. I remember sleeping in bunk beds, trying to time my breathing to the seven others in the room, trying to make their snores my own.

Talley tells me she has a special treat for us.

I feel embarrassed because I think she's going to give me another present. She sets up my computer. She puts on *Helter Skelter*. I've never seen it. I know who Charles Manson is; the comparisons the media made between The Survivors and The Family were false but everywhere. She gives me two Swedish Fish infused with THC. I eat them. The movie has all the seventies trappings of bad acting and too-loud music and scenes that could've been a sentence instead of a ten-minute conversation. I'm stoned watching a man I don't find charismatic in the slightest give a bad name to groups of people living among loving families of their own choosing.

At one point, Talley tells me she totally would've joined The Family.

She gives a stoned laugh. I let it be. She says, "Serious. Sit around all day doing drugs and having sex…what's not to like about that?"

"It's not real," I say.

"What's *real* anyway?"

"Love."

"Exactly. Like Manson said."

"He was selfish. He only wanted people to love *him*. Same with all the others. All of them preaching about being the Second Coming and all of that. That's not real."

"Obviously."

"No, not that he actually wasn't the Second Coming, but the entire premise. It's false. Nothing good comes from worship. Nothing."

"You hate God."

"If there was one."

"What happened to you as a child?"

"I'm just saying, any group set up to place a single person above all else is doomed to fail."

"But not your precious Survivors."

"They're not—"

"Why don't you marry them?"

"Oh my God you're annoying when you're high."

"Get a room."

"Let's watch something else."

"Okay, okay, I'll be quiet." Talley rights herself so she sits against the wall. She pulls my head into her lap. She traces her index finger along the ridge of my ear.

We watch a naked woman with blond hair smoke a joint. My heartbeat slows back down.

"You know," Talley says, "for a guy who's all about Honesty, you sure as fuck are guarded."

"I'm shy."

"You're not. You pretend to be, but you're not."

"I'm an open book."

"Right. An open book who has no past."

"Whatever."

"Who hurt you?"

I speak without guarding myself: "My father."

"What'd he do?"

"The usual things fathers do."

"Hit you?"

"I try not to live in victimhood."

"Right, because you're practically a disciple of Dr. Sick. Don't forget I read that shit, too."

"What good does it do?"

"Guess so."

"No, really," I say. "What good is thinking about all that? So I can feel wronged? Misunderstood? Righteous in my anger? What good does any of that do?"

"It's part of being human."

"Not a part I'm interested in."

"Then what are you interested in? That's maybe what I'm asking. What, Mason Hues, gets you excited?"

"This spectacular apartment."

Talley laughs. She hits my chest. She tells me she's serious.

"I don't know."

She puts her hand to my face. She presses until I look up at her. A tiny flake of crust is suspended in her right nostril. I understand she wants me to tell her that *she* makes me excited. But then the skin connecting her ear loosens and I understand she's moved on from selfish wants and genuinely wants to know something about me.

I sit up. I press my back to the wall. I cross my legs. I tell her to do the same. She asks what I'm doing and I tell her I'm giving her a gift. She laughs. I say I am giving her a gift that was given to me. She tells me she's not into anal, but appreciates the sentiment.

"Okay," she says.

"I need you to respond with as much Honesty as you can possibly muster. Do not filter your answers. Respond with the first thing that comes to your mind. Let the words flow from you. Open yourself up to this experience."

Talley nods.

Nothing about this practice is in *Dr. Sick* or anywhere else. Nobody spoke about what happened in Marble. The only information anyone had came from my testimonies, and I hadn't mentioned this.

"One last thing," I say.

"Yeah?"

"I need you to speak directly into my ear."

"For real?"

"For real."

I lean my head toward Talley. I feel the heat radiating off of her face. Her lips don't touch my ear, but they're close. I ask her to describe her first love to me. She doesn't say the boy she'd told me about outside of A Fine Line; she tells me about her father. She tells me about being a little girl and running to him after he got home from work. She was a dog, anxious every time he left the house, worried she'd never see him again. She tells me about sitting in his lap in the den. How he always wore button-down shirts with the top two left undone. How she'd wedge her ear between the cotton and press it against his hairy chest. How this tickled. How she could hear his heartbeat. How sometimes it seemed to skip a beat and she'd cry because she thought her father was going to die.

I ask her about her favorite memory. Her mouth rolls moisture into my ear. She tells me about a trip they'd taken, her family, her two brothers and mom and dad. They drove from Illinois to Wyoming. She'd gotten sick, really sick. First her throat and then her stomach, vomiting and tears, strep. They'd rented a motel room in Cody. The pool had sharks painted on its bottom. They'd been tired after going to urgent care, so they bought dinner from a gas station. She'd eaten pretzels and cream cheese. They'd watched *Twister*. Her whole family sat in a small room on two beds with the lights low and they were together and quiet and safe. They'd been kind to Talley, loving. It felt like family.

I ask about her biggest regret.

Her lips press against my skin and she inhales with a catch and then I feel wetness from her tears. I fight to stay in the moment, to not filter this experience through my own. I am only partially successful. Talley tells me about her first serious boyfriend, Peter Daniels, a pretty boy who loved drugs and her with an equal desperation. She'd been older and went to college across the country while he finished his senior year. She tells me she hadn't meant to become infatuated with Sean, a junior at DU, but it'd happened, innocently at first, parties and movies and conversations that seemed to hit upon a level she'd never been able to access with Peter. A stolen kiss. A drunken blowjob. Then it was constant and it was passionate and it felt wrong but it felt more right or maybe she simply didn't care. Peter's life was falling apart with his discovery of opiates. He was kicked out of school. He ran away, showed up in Denver, cried into her arms. He had no idea what to do. He told her he couldn't stop thinking about killing himself. Talley tells me she watched a boy she'd loved shoot drugs and pass out. She slipped out of her dorm to go see Sean. She cried to him about not knowing what to do. The mirroring of the situations felt like a worse betrayal than the sex they had afterward.

Talley quits speaking.

Her breathing is the mucus-coated labors of the hysterical.

I turn. I take the back of her head. I press my forehead to hers. Our whites accept one another. I know she's experiencing what everybody does when they first recognize the cornerstones of their characters. I know she feels light, free, able to breathe for perhaps the first time in her life. I am giving her the gift that One gave me. And this excites me or makes me feel whole or at least like I'm once again living in Honesty.

# 12. SICK (III)

I'd wake up from fitful sleeps with the cotton sheets clinging to my body. I'd experience a sense of panic from the pressure and constriction, claustrophobia so acute I'd scream. Somebody would always be there. They would kneel beside me, helping free me from the soaked sheets. They'd tell me to take deep breaths. They'd rub my head. On my third week of treatment, this exact scenario was occurring, Twenty at my side, his emaciated face staring down at me, his right hand stroking. The moon shone through the blinds. His hand was furry, slick with my sweat, covered in my poisoned hair.

# 13. MASON HUES

One always said that trying to replicate a past experience was one of the most crushing endeavors a person can put himself through. He said the experience obviously could never be the same. He said the person trying to recreate this moment is struck by the fleeting notion of time's great power, which, for most, results in feeling his own mortality.

I'm thinking about this at A Fine Line.

Derek's band is back on stage and I'm not rolling or high so their music is just loud and annoying. I don't feel much like dancing. Talley must be feeling the same thing. She tries to dance but doesn't seem that into it and the whole night feels like a bummer.

We outgrow experiences even before they are over.

We are granted the curse of consciousness, once an asset in assessing danger, but now without actual threats, it has become a virus multiplying self-centered thoughts about things that shouldn't matter. Everything becomes hypothetical. Everything is Prince Charming slipping on glass slippers to our different futures.

Every religion and spiritual practice is designed to break this cycle. To grant us a single moment of being in the present.

The band goes on set break. I think about leaving but Talley comes back from the bar with two drinks and we sit at a wooden high-top. She complains about the crowd being low energy. I agree. Whiskey burns my throat.

"I don't know," she says. "Maybe it's just me who's low energy."

"Maybe."

"Or like over this whole scene."

"It wouldn't hurt for them to add a new song or two."

Talley smiles even though I can tell she doesn't want to. "You ever just get really fucking sick of your life?"

I think about being incarcerated in one form or another for thirty months. I nod.

"Need like an adventure or something."

"I'll pretend not to take offense," I say.

"I'm not sick of *you*."

"What aren't you getting?"

"I don't know. It's just...same shit, same people, same scene. I'm over it."

"That's not what I asked."

"What am I not getting?"

"Yeah."

Talley looks like she's about to give a real answer, one aspiring to Honesty, when she smiles. "I'll tell you what *you're* not getting, but are about to."

"Huh?"

"Laid."

"What?"

"Because that dude over there is giving you the up-and-down-and-all-around."

I follow her gaze. That's when I see a kid I know, Joshua Smith, a kid I'd grown up with in Boulder. He's a little fatter than when I'd known him at fifteen. He has a lip ring and a mess of gelled hair. He stares at me and we make eye contact and then he smiles and starts in our direction. I don't know what to do. I need to not have been seen and I need these worlds to stay separate and I need to get out of the bar and then he's at the side of our table.

"Mason?"

"Hey, what's up?"

"Dude, what the fuck? Where…how are you?"

"I'm good."

"What are you doing?"

"Here for the band."

"No, I mean, like what happened to you? Where have you been?"

He obviously doesn't know where I'd really gone at fifteen—my parents don't even know—but he might have heard I'd been locked up. Boulder is small. Adults with money all talked about how great their kids were, but even more so, they talked about the kids who fucked everything up. He would've heard something. And he's stupid enough to drag some version of it out in front of Talley.

"Just hanging out," I say.

Joshua tilts his head. His lips part. There's a moment where he seems to understand I want him to let it be, but the moment is fleeting. He says, "I heard you—"

"Not true," I say.

"Were locked up," he says.

I glance across the table at Talley, who smiles with her mouth but not her eyes.

I have to give a version of Honesty.

I say, "Yeah, that happened. Was sweet, I assure you."

"What'd you do?"

"Breaking and entering."

"What?"

"Had a little habit going. Needed money to support it. I was popped for a series of B and E's. End of story."

"Dude, you straight up vanished. Gone. Nobody knew what happened."

"That's what happened."

"But your parents didn't even know what happened. I saw your mom like two months ago. She said she had no idea where you were."

I cringe. I can't look at Talley.

"Oh well," I say.

"Crazy. So crazy. Mason Hues. I can't believe you're…alive."

"I'm sorry," Talley says. "We weren't introduced."

Joshua turns to Talley. He sizes her up, then sticks out his hand. "Joshua. I went to school with Mason before he pulled a Houdini."

"Talley."

"Sally?"

"With a T."

"Nice to meet you."

"You too."

She lets go of his hand. Joshua stands there like an idiot. He reaches into his pocket and pulls out his phone. "Dude, you have to let me get a pic with you. Proof, man."

"Fuck off," Talley says.

Joshua looks at her like he'd just been spit on.

"Serious. Get the fuck out of here," she says.

"I didn't mean—"

"Fuck. Off."

Joshua looks at me and then back to Talley. He shakes his head and starts walking away. I stand. I am about to start apologizing, but no words come out. I walk toward the exit. I need to be alone and I need quiet. I've ruined everything. I've lied. I've predicated our relationship upon the death of my parents. I've never mentioned having disappeared. I've never mentioned being incarcerated. I've never mentioned anything real.

I'm outside. I'm going to be alone. I can't go back to isolation. I can't stand not being touched.

"Mason!"

I keep walking. I hear footsteps behind me and then Talley grabs my arm and I stop and she looks more confused than angry.

"What the fuck?" she says.

"What?"

"*What*? What do you mean *what*?"

Cars inch by with bar traffic. I feel like a spectacle.

"Say something. Anything. But just start talking."

I've gone eight months without saying a single word. Part of this was because I had nothing to say. Part of this was because the psych ward was better than being called a faggot in juvie. But perhaps the largest part of this silence was the guilt of having already talked too much. Talked to the wrong people. Talked to those with the power to make consequences disappear. I'd talked about One. I'd talked about Five. I'd talked about The Day of Gifts. I'd talked about everything in order to reduce my suffering. I'd put myself above my family.

"Who the fuck are you?" Talley says.

I stare at her. I understand that I'd had it wrong before; she does not need a project and she doesn't need somebody to talk to and she doesn't need somebody to validate her life. She needs Honesty.

Maybe she's one of the few who can actually shoulder its burden.

Maybe there are no accidents.

Maybe I'd received enough confidence from my new haircut to walk into Talley's Tatters. Maybe I'd been led to somebody who searched with an open desperation for Truth. Maybe we'd become friends because our True Selves recognized this in one another. And maybe we'd run into Joshua Smith because lies could only take us so far. Maybe it was the universe's way of breaking the shackles of deceit. Maybe we were supposed to have this moment, as I'd had when I put my face to the glass of a strange mansion in the woods and saw a man and woman with bald heads hold one another.

"Thirty-Seven," I say.

"What the fuck are you talking about?"

My body thrums with energy. Tingles and heat, pressure, buoyancy. It's like the gift One had given me the first night on the boulder, like the gift I had given Talley while sitting on my bed. It's the initial sliver of bliss resulting from Honesty.

"I am Thirty-Seven."

"Years old? What the fuck are you…" Talley's voice trails off. Her hand goes to her mouth. Her eyes widen and headlights light them up and I think she looks beautiful in her vulnerability of understanding. "You're such a fucking liar," she says. But her words are soft, a question, a plea for me to be lying.

One always said that if a person says he was sorry, he needed to be one hundred percent committed to never repeating the same action.

"I'm sorry," I say. "About lying. About deceiving you."

Talley shakes her head. She steps back. The skin connecting her ear is tight. I extend my hand and touch her arm.

"Stay the fuck away from me."

"Talley."

"No, fuck you."

A group of drunk frat boys walks by and laughs.

"Talley."

She doesn't respond. She walks away and then starts to jog. I feel like crying. I am alone. The drunk guys make fun of me. I worry she'll tell somebody. I try to calm myself by thinking she won't say anything because she isn't that type of girl and because I know how people work. This feels true. I know it will take time, as it had with me. I know those who search for Truth eventually find it.

# 14. SICK (IV)

They worried about my weight loss. I couldn't keep anything down, not even liquids. One lowered my dose of Cytoxan. I was grateful for this act of kindness. I'd originally been outfitted with medium-sized black scrubs. After three weeks, I was fitting into an extra small. Five spoon-fed me rice and when I couldn't swallow solids, she switched to chicken broth. I wanted to leave the cabin. I wanted Monday mornings with their IV bags to die. I hated everything.

That first month was the worst month of my life.

I'd lie there all day, trying my hardest not to move. The nausea was an unrelenting hurricane, each pulse a nation-destroying wall of sick. People held cold cloths to my head. I had an accident while I vomited into a bucket. Twenty-Two gave me a sponge bath. I didn't care that his soap-covered hands scrubbed my genitals. I slept all the time because it was easier. I never felt rested. Sometimes I would smell my breath against the pillow, which would immediately send a gag ricocheting through my throat.

I could see every one of my ribs.

My eyes were sunken, just like the others.

One night One came into the largest of the dorms. I was curled in a ball on a bottom bunk. I was on day two of my week, so the sicks were strong. He knelt down. I couldn't smile because the pressure would hurt my teeth. He placed his hand on my forehead.

"You're really warm," he said.

I stared at a man who was killing me.

"You've done so well. You really have." He stroked my bald head. "Your search will bear tremendous gifts."

"Kill me."

One didn't move. He stroked my head and stared at me and I was pretty sure he'd heard me, pretty sure he understood I was willing to die, *ready* to die, ready to do anything to stop the suffering.

"All you have to do is say *stop*."

"Stop."

"Does your True Self want this, or does Mason Hues?"

"It's the same thing."

"What is gained by stopping? What do you have? Where will you go? What is better than building a family who is and has gone through exactly what you have?"

"I want to die."

One lowered a little so his butt rested against the backs of his legs. Elvis played from the main room. People laughed. Nobody was as sick as me. Nobody was as young and they probably had messed up the dose and I was going to die before I could drive a car.

"I had a little girl," One said. "She was your age, maybe a few years younger. She got sick. I sat by her for months at a time. I stroked her hairless head, just like I am doing to you. She was the sole thing in life that gave me joy."

I blinked. A tear fell; they were always falling without me knowing why.

"One night, she told me she was ready. That was all she said. I asked her what she meant. She turned around and faced the wall. I got angry. I told her she was being selfish. That it was hell on our whole family. I told her she owed it to me to keep fighting. I said I would never forgive her if she gave up."

One wasn't crying, but close.

"My daughter died that night."

His rubbing of my head started back up.

"That was my biggest regret. It cost me my marriage, my career, and nearly my life. I spent so many nights hating myself for letting my fear and selfishness force my actions into the ugliest sort."

"Wasn't your fault."

"I was steeped in fear and want. I was a prisoner to my own mortal self. I couldn't see Truth in anything. But through this work we're doing here, I was finally able to see that moment for exactly what it was: my daughter had reached a level of Honesty that I will forever aspire to. At that moment she told me she was ready, she accepted the falsity of human desire to thwart mortality. She was giving me the gift of seeing an example of Perfect Honesty."

I didn't know what to say and I hurt and I was crying and I wanted to rescue his daughter and I wanted to be rescued.

"So I will ask you this question one time, and respect your wishes, as I did not do with my own daughter: Do you want to die?"

"No."

"Do you want to leave?"

"No."

"Do you want to live in Honesty amongst a loving family of your choosing?"

"Yes."[5]

---

5 According to *Dr. Sick: The Survivors and The Day of Gifts*, Dr. James Shepard had been married for seventeen years. He and his wife, Patti, had a single daughter, Zoe. She developed lymphoma shortly after turning thirteen. She battled this cancer at Denver Medical Center, the hospital where her father worked as an oncologist. After nearly two years of battling, Zoe Rose Shepard passed away in the Shepards'

mountain home. Henry O'Connor writes, "The irony, of course, was devastating: the nationally renowned Dr. James Shepard—a man who saved countless others from the grips of cancer—could do nothing for his own daughter. It is no great assumption to see this as the moment when Shepard's mental crack became something of a fissure. Soon, everything around him slipped off its crumbling surface. Down and down it went—his illustrious career, his marriage, his fragile relationship with morality—everything imploding into the vortex of anger at the injustices of life."

# 15. SICK (V)

Two things happened during my second month:
1) My treatments lessened to once every two weeks
2) Thirty-Eight arrived

I was finally able to have a series of days when I wasn't vomiting. I was able to drink fluids and even swallow small bits of rice. I was able to get up in the morning. I was able to sit on the deck with a wool blanket wrapped around my shoulders and talk with the others. I could almost see how beautiful everything around me was. And strangely, I liked how I looked. I liked the fact I was nothing but bones and I liked the fact my head was always cold and I liked the fact everything was too big. I felt pretty, or at least like I was no different from the others.

Then Thirty-Eight showed up. He was an older man, probably close to fifty. He rang the doorbell. We all stopped. I sat on the couch with Five. She taught me Cat's Cradle. We looked up to see Thirty-Eight's shape. I was scared it was my father or the police or some other male authority figure who was bent on doing bad things. One walked through the living room. He opened the door a crack.

"James."

"Bob? My God, it's good to see you." One stepped outside. I could see the old guy peering over One's shoulder, a look of confused panic on his face.

Five told me we should go downstairs. I followed. The rest of us gathered down there. A few of us were worried because One had obviously known this man, but the man sure hadn't looked like he'd known what we were up to. Somebody said there was nothing to worry about; there were no accidents. Somebody else said that we could be arrested. For what? For the administration of controlled substances. For attempted murder. There are no accidents. One will know what to do. I'm scared. Don't live in fear.

One was gone for a long time.

We sat there in the basement listening to Elvis, helping those who were struggling, pretending we weren't terrified of what was occurring outside of our doors. It was close to eight o'clock when we heard the back door finally open. We all looked up the stairs. We waited. One walked down.

He looked stern and he looked old and he maybe looked worried. But then he smiled.

We let out a communal sigh.

"Thirty-Eight is still searching. His search led him here. He was looking for the man I used to be, one he knew had experienced the loss of a loved one. But he found the man I now am. He will be back."

Three weeks went by, and then there was a knocking at our door. One answered. Thirty-Eight stood there with a small duffle bag. His eyes were rimmed red with tears. He stared at us and then One took hold of the back of Thirty-Eight's head and pressed his forehead against his and I smiled because it was beautiful, the relief I could see washing over Thirty-Eight, his shoulders heaving with sobs, the gift of the first sliver of living in Honesty.

I liked Thirty-Eight.

He was kind and broken and quiet.

Being the newest member of the family, I became his Big Brother. I showed him around. We hiked a half mile, at which point I got sick and nearly collapsed. He held me. He wanted to be of use. He wanted to be needed. I leaned against his old body on the walk back home. I allowed him to speak to me about his past, as One told me was allowed during his first two weeks. He'd been a partner at Denver Medical Center. He'd been a radiologist. His marriage fell apart when his youngest son became addicted to opiates, going through the revolving door of treatments and sober living facilities and relapses, and now was homeless, somewhere, anywhere, going on nine months, maybe dead. He said he hadn't known what to do. He said he'd thought of James, the tragic loss he'd gone through, and had driven out here guided by the faintest memory of visiting the cabin some twenty years before.

I fought the selfish need for Thirty-Eight to be my father.

I pressed my forehead to his. We looked in the whites of one another's eyes.

After two weeks, we sat around a fire. The second snow of the season fell. I sat next to Thirty-Eight. I rubbed his back. One stood. He made eye contact with each and every one of us. Thirty-Eight stood. I helped Five undress him. She motioned for me to take hold of his arm. I cradled his elbow and wrist and snow fell and One inserted a needle and then I held the plastic bag above my head and we clapped and we were warm and happy or at least content.

I nursed Thirty-Eight through his first month.

I hardly ever left his side, always with a cup of Pedialyte and a cold washcloth. Always there to tell him I was proud. Always there to tell him he was doing well. Always there to say we all loved him.

In his third week, he told me he wanted to die.

I knelt by the bottom bunk. I stroked his paper-thin hair. I told him about growing up in a house with a father who pleasured himself in my doorway while he thought I was asleep. I told him I'd wanted nothing more than a father who loved me. I told him I was tortured with knowing my father's actions were wrong, but wanting to take part in them, if only for the physical contact I could perceive as love. I told him I ran away. I told him I came here. I told him I'd never been happier. I'd never felt more loved. I'd never felt more capable of love. I said that each day I thought less and less about the loss in my life, less and less about myself.

Thirty-Eight cried.

I started stroking his head again.

I told him each person had their own journey; some of them led to Honesty, some of them led to deceit. I said his own son was in the midst of this journey. Thirty-Eight blinked in the form of a nod. I told him I would have given anything to have such a loving man as my father. I told him I was grateful to have the chance to choose him as part of my loving family.

We were silent.

I said, "I'll ask you this once, and only once, understood?"

He nodded.

"Do you want to die?"

"No."

"Do you want to leave?"

"I don't know."

"Do you want to live in Honesty with a loving family of your choosing?"

Thirty-Eight tried to smile. I knelt forward and kissed his forehead. He smelled like rotting cheese and grape-flavored drink. I didn't care. He clasped his fingers through mine. He closed his eyes. I held his hand until he was granted the gift of sleep.

# 16. REPRIEVE

This story isn't about drugs. Not Cytoxan or DMT.[6]

---

6 Henry O'Connor writes extensively about the use of *N,N*-Dimethyltrypt-amine among The Survivors. He dedicates two chapters of *Dr. Sick* to this very topic. He makes outlandish claims about the drug's importance in Dr. James Shepard's teachings. He paints pictures that aren't true by writing *I imagine* as a subtle preface. Of course he connects our use of DMT to sex, which is ridiculous to anyone who has actually taken the drug; for several infinite minutes, there is no reality outside of your mind's eye.

I imagine this fraction of our story has a certain flashy appeal. It gives a causal relationship to what happened later. It probably helped sell the pitch. I don't blame Henry O'Connor because somewhere near the heart of his book is the search for Truth. He asks important questions. It's not his fault he's steeped in want of literary acclaim, which happens to be the subject his fallacies have rooted themselves in, propagating the notion of their arrival bringing happiness.

Perhaps O'Connor's real obsession with Reprieve is the paper trail it left of James and the rest of us. For a group operating in peaceful harmony for close to three years, a group living in a home with running utilities and paid taxes, a family which multiplied through happenstance and murmurs from sick mouths, there was hardly any information about what occurred inside of those angular glass-covered walls. Really, there was only the information from the DEA, and then my testimony. There was a paper trail connecting James to YYCIM Laboratories in Hoboken, New Jersey. And when YYCIM was raided—a single brick building left over from the American industry days of leather tanning, three employees total (a chemist, a shipper, and a bookkeeper)—and electronic ledgers were discovered, decoded, and pursued, Dr. James Shepard's name became a very small blip on the DEA's screen. Three different shipments of two ounces of DMT were sent to a Denver condo, one owned by Shepard, one none of us knew about. The DEA had much bigger concerns with other YYCIM clients; the amount shipped to Shepard was a laughable joke, one not worth the manpower of sending a single county deputy up the roads of Marble, Colorado, to investigate.

But it was *something*.

Something O'Connor could use his questionable journalistic skills to investigate. Something that gave causes. Something that formed the types of stereotypes both he and the public fostered regarding "cults." Drugs and sex. Mind control. Felonies on top of felonies. Fire. Hedonism. Pedophilia. Polygamy. Why? Because this is the easier way. This is a way that keeps those reading safe. Their constructed walls of lies, wants, and fears are reinforced with this mental picture of drug-fueled orgies. They know they are not the type to experiment with heavy psychedelics. Heavy psychedelics are used in brainwashing; therefore, they are not the type to be brainwashed.

Modus ponens.

Everybody wants to infer Truth.

This version is so much easier to understand than a group of people finding one another and building lives based on the search for Truth amongst a loving family of their own choosing.

We don't fear the cliff—we fear jumping.

How much easier is it to tell your children to stay away from drugs than to stay away from people who question the reason over half of marriages end in divorce, who wonder why one in five girls and one in twenty boys are sexually abused, who can't wrap their heads around the notion of buying bigger and more exclusive homes in order to isolate us even further when all we want is to be touched in nonsexual ways.

O'Connor knew the name Dr. James Shepard gave to our monthly ingesting of DMT. He writes, "Reprieve: to cancel or postpone the punishment of (someone, someone especially condemned to death). It is hard to imagine a more apt naming for The Survivors' hallucinogenic ceremonies. Here they were, literally being killed by a man who claimed to be their savior [Never once did One claim to be anything close to a *savior*], only to believe this moment of dissociation caused by DMT to be a gift, when in fact, it further cemented them into mental servitude to Shepard, further placing him on the pedestal of Celestial Other."

This, of course, is bullshit.

We knew what DMT was. Some of us had done it. We knew any insights gained from the experience had originated in ourselves. We knew it did not matter who gave us the drug. We knew all of these things, yet we still called it *Reprieve*.

The truth is, we liked it.

We felt deserving of it.

Those not sick from their Cytoxan dose sometimes fornicated.

We always smoked it sitting by a fire.

Sometimes we saw God.

Sometimes we remembered there was no such thing.

Sometimes we cried and begged to be held.

Sometimes we imagined the people who had been charged with loving us actually doing just that.

I don't remember telling the Feds anything about Reprieve.

One always said that if somebody tells you they don't remember doing something, they may not, in fact, remember taking the action, but they always remember the exact moment a decision was made.

My first Reprieve came after nearly eight weeks. I'd smoked weed and drank before, but nothing harder. I was excited. Everybody else was too. Thirty-Eight was too sick to partake, but he sat next to me and Five. It was sometime in October. Most of the leaves had fallen and the air was thick with cold and smoke and my hands shook with the tin foil. I didn't want to embarrass myself. I took three hits.

I understand everyone has a different experience on DMT. I understand this to be true about all psychedelic substances. This only makes sense; we have different issues we're trying to work through. We have different brain chemistry. We have different susceptibilities.

But maybe that's only true for people in the world where they're living in constant efforts to fortify themselves from Truth.

Because we were connected.

Everything was connected.

Everything was a single mind, us tiny bits of energy exploding through a red and yellow vortex of molecular biology, strobes of light, the weightlessness of being propelled over synaptic gaps, tendrils of energy that looked so much like love.

One told us that any insights we gathered during Reprieve were inherently True. He said they were gifts. He said when done once a month, DMT provided the extra energy to break down walls that were created while we were still in utero.

I remember my first epiphany well: Honesty is the most synergistic force in the universe; it can, and will, change the world.

O'Connor writes, "Any grouping of individuals experiencing a traumatic experience with fatal consequences, only to be 'saved,' develop an overly dependent relationship upon their savior. There are countless examples of this relationship throughout our history—a platoon being rescued; those stranded being excavated; chronic sufferers of debilitating mental or physical disorders becoming fixated on their doctors or therapists, often sexualizing this relationship to a detrimental level—and The Survivors are no exception. They were dying and Dr. James Shepard gave them a gift. The gift brought them back to life, and therefore, in a form of delusional modus ponens, the dying equated Dr. James Shepard to renewed life. With this in mind, it is possible to give this ritual another name: *revival: restoration of force, validity, or effect*. In essence, Dr. James Shepard took his followers' lives, destroyed them, and gave them back through a psychotropic drug. The Survivors received their same lives back, yet these lives felt different compared to the hell they had been enduring. Dr. James Shepard repackaged their lives, placing himself in the role of Savior, month after month, a primal form of behavioral modification through punishment and reward, a process that all but guaranteed a fanatical devotion."

# 17. CULPABLE

Thirty-Eight's spirits lowered every day. His desire to live drained with every injection. He made it through his first month, but even dropping to biweekly doses didn't help. He slept when he should've felt well enough to sit with us on the patio. He started talking about his family more and more. He talked about his wife, whom he had become convinced he could win back. He droned on and on about his son, if he was alive, if he needed Thirty-Eight's help. He said something about being a coward for running from his problems.

We all noticed.

We tried not to talk about it because that was slander and slander was a form of character assassination and character assassination was an easy crutch to deflect an Honest gaze at one's own self.

But we talked all the same.

I overheard Five and One talking one afternoon. I scrubbed the sink while they whispered. Five said Thirty-Eight's attitude was bringing people down. She said it was a cancer. She said it couldn't go on like this. One pressed his forehead to hers and this made me jealous. He told her some people fought against Honesty more than others, but sickness made a believer out of everyone.

I tried to be extra kind to Thirty-Eight. I lay next to him and sometimes told him stories and sometimes just kept quiet. I bathed him. He experienced his first Reprieve in November and even that didn't help. He just kept crying.

Sometime around Thanksgiving he started telling me he wanted to die again. He looked me straight in the eye and said he was ready. I nodded. I left to go find One. He was in the master bedroom, which he kept locked. I told him Thirty-Eight was saying that he wanted to die.

"We all say things we don't mean when engulfed in selfish fear."

"I know," I said. "But I think he means it."

"And you know this *how*?"

"I...I don't. He seemed serious, is all."

One looked at me and then his face was back to how it normally appeared—warmth in the eyes, his nostrils relaxed—and he put his hand behind my head and we pressed our foreheads and he thanked me for bringing this matter to his attention; he would have a talk with Thirty-Eight.

Later that afternoon, I was with Five on the couch. She pressed against each of my vertebrae, pausing, telling me a story of each of their lives. We saw One and Thirty-Eight emerge from a bedroom. They were dressed for outside. I didn't want Thirty-Eight to make eye contact with me because he would've known I'd tattled. They walked outside.

"Thank God," Five said. "It's about time he got his shit together."

"Where are they going?"

"Probably the boulder. Have a heart-to-heart. A chance for re-dedication. And if Thirty-Eight can't get back on board, One will send him on his way."

I nodded. Five pressed on the next nub of my spine. She told me this little guy was a fighter, real scrappy. She told me he came from nothing, but unlike everyone else in the world, he wanted to remain as nothing. I waited for her story to continue, but she moved on to my next vertebrae.

An hour or so later, One walked in through the patio door. I was dusting. One was alone. He didn't smile when we met eyes and then he walked to the kitchen and opened the cupboard and pulled out a handheld bell the size of a softball. He closed his eyes as if steeling himself against the sound or maybe the act itself. He rang the bell.

I had no idea what was going on.

A few people ran down the hallway from the rooms. They appeared panicked, in need of guidance. One kept ringing. More people rushed into the main room. Something wasn't right. Twenty-One leaned against the wall, a bucket in his hand, sweat covering his naked body. I knew he'd received his shot the previous morning because I'd given it to him. If he was out of bed, something was horribly wrong.

One set the bell down. The ringing muted itself instantly. It was then I noticed his hands. They trembled. They were covered in red.

Thirty-six of us stood in the kitchen and family room looking at One.

"Today," One said, "I have seen the power of what we are up against."

Twenty-One wretched into his bucket. One waited for him to finish. Nobody helped Twenty-One because we were all too scared.

"I have seen the power of selfish fear and selfish want firsthand. I have seen a small fraction of what it is capable of."

One held up his hands. A few of us cried.

"I watched a man refuse to carry on with the work of breaking down Self. I watched a man choose the Big Lie over Truth."

I didn't understand.

I understood just fine, I simply didn't want to understand.

"Nothing happens by accident. Nothing. Not because there's some Czar of the Heavens, but because everything that occurs has the capacity to be a learning moment. Everything relates back to the search for Truth. Everything—even the tragic—can bring us closer to Honesty."

Thirty-Eight was dead. He had jumped instead of continued on. He was a coward. I hoped he found peace. I hoped he was in more pain. I thought of fathers always failing, no matter the circumstances.

"This is on all of us," One said. "We all will take part in his disposal."

Thirty-Eight lay face down at the bottom of the boulder where I'd decided to embark upon my search for Truth a few months prior. Bone stuck through his right elbow. A pool of blood had melted the snow underneath his head. His one eye I could see was open. I stared into its whites and I told myself the whites couldn't lie and maybe his couldn't because I noticed the back of his bald head was caved in and I thought that was strange because he'd obviously fallen the other way.

We loaded Thirty-Eight into a wheelbarrow.

A lot of us cried as we hiked through the mountains.

The sun was close to setting and it was cold and some of us got sick and I wondered if it was because of our treatments or seeing a family member dead.

One brought us a few miles into the woods. We made our way to the cliffs. We veered away and down until we were covered by pines and then it was black out. Some of us carried shovels. We started digging. The first foot was easy and then it wasn't. When it was my turn, I tried to be strong. My hands sprouted blisters, then blood. We all took turns. Three feet down we hit granite. One told us that was enough.

We understood this was what had to be done.

We drank grape Pedialyte.

We understood this was the only way to ensure our safety. This was the only way we could keep living in Honesty with a loving family of our own choosing.

One walked over to the wheelbarrow. He held a large pair of pliers. He tapped them against his black pants. He looked down at dead Thirty-Eight and then back at us.

"Some of us are not strong enough for this journey. I want you to look at this man and realize it could easily have been you. Any of us. Any single one of us has felt, at one point or another, it would be easier to kill ourselves. This is all of us."

We nodded and sniffled and rubbed our freezing hands together.

"Just as this man is all of us, so too is his burial. We are all complicit in his death. We are all complicit in not being strong enough to help guide him to Honesty. We are all culpable to his selfish actions."

One put his hand on Thirty-Eight's jaw. He pried open his mouth. He grunted and yanked and then there was more blood and One straightened and held up the pliers, a tooth so close to the whites of Thirty-Eight's dead eye.

"I will call those of you in need of this experience to do as I've done. You will be in charge of this tooth, this reminder of what lies are capable of causing. You will file it down every day until it is dust. Then, and only then, will you have fully grasped the severity of this death."

Nobody said a word.

One pulled out a sheet of tin foil and a baggie of DMT. It wasn't a Reprieve night. One spoke to this fact: "Those I call upon will be rewarded with a Reprieve after the act is completed. This will help internalize the Absolute Truth that is death."

Thirty pulled the second tooth.

We stood and shivered.

We hoped we'd be left alone; we hoped we'd be chosen.

Twenty-One and then Three and then Twenty-Five.

They were given their Reprieve with blood-soaked hands.

I stood taller.

I felt ashamed at my selfishness for wanting to be included.

Thirty-Four and Five and Nineteen.

One looked directly at me. It was too dark to see anything but his whites. He called my name, Thirty-Seven, and I smiled.

The only teeth left were molars.

I kept gouging his gums.

I felt the shudders of roots ripping through my entire body.

The tooth was like nothing I'd ever seen before. It had a tail, a cone-like bottom because it hadn't died on its own.

One gave me my Reprieve. I held the glass stem stained red with the others' bloody fingerprints. On my third inhale, I fell backward into the snow. I surfed upon a communal consciousness. Everything was shades of red until it was blinding white, a color I knew was Thirty-Eight's eyes. I arrived at Truth. The eyes told me. They told me he hadn't jumped. He'd been beaten over the head with a rock and then pushed off the cliff because he'd questioned One, told him this whole thing had gone too far. *James, this has to stop.* But this wasn't the real Truth. The real Truth was that this act needed to happen. Because regardless of what One said, nobody could leave. We'd chosen a loving family. Because we were all we had. Because once a single person left, it was over with, the harmony of those surviving.

There was one Truth even deeper, one I fought toward with all of my might as the tentacles of consciousness clawed their way back into my mind's eye: by ripping out Thirty-Eight's tooth, I was as guilty as One in this old man's murder. And I was okay with that. I was more than okay with that. I was excited to have been chosen.

# 18. TWO

Three weeks pass with no word from Talley. I don't go into work because I know she would just yell and tell me to leave. I don't do much of anything during that time besides meet with my PO. I tell him lies that he knows are lies, but he doesn't question them because it's easier. I feel alone in a bad way. I worry about Joshua Smith telling everyone in Boulder that he'd seen me. I tell myself it doesn't matter, that nothing matters. Sometimes this feels okay. I wonder why my parents haven't tried to track me down.

I read *Dr. Sick* with an orange highlighter.

I watch Netflix.

I eat rice and drink Mr. Pibb.

I tell myself she'll come back because there are no accidents and then I tell myself there are accidents all the time and nothing One said ever held up over the long haul.

But on the twenty-third day, there's a frantic pounding on my door. It's the middle of the night. I climb out of bed. I wear only boxers. I press my face to the keyhole and see Talley and it takes a second for me to compose myself and quit smiling. Talley barely seems to register me. She clomps around my apartment in her clunky boots. She wears a purple wig and a miniskirt and her face is the sloppy of the crying or the drunk. She finally speaks—*stop looking at me*—and I realize she's been doing both.

I don't say anything.

I understand she needs to feel some sense of control. This moment has not been planned, and probably wouldn't have happened had she not been drunk, but she still needs a sense of power. She needs to vent. She needs to inflate her sense of Self. I'm okay with this.

But I'm not expecting what she says: "Are you even gay?"

"I don't know."

"You don't know? You don't know? You either like dick or not. Pretty straightforward."

"I have been with a man."

"Bullshit."

"But I would not consider myself homosexual."

Talley shakes her head. She's about to say something, but she just shakes her head more vehemently. She paces. She makes her fingers into a sharpened point, which she wields in my direction. She says, "That's practically rape. Like…" She points to my bed on the floor. "All that shit we did on there. Here you were getting off on it the whole time."

I am mute.

"Pathological," Talley says. "A complete pathological liar. You are, you know that?"

"I lie no more than anyone else."

"Oh my fucking God, are you serious? Because I can tell you with one hundred percent certainty that I've never lied to you, at least nothing big."

"Nobody can be Honest all of the time."

"Shut the fuck up with your bullshit. Listen to yourself. You're crazy. Absolutely crazy."

"I do not believe myself so."

"Only crazy people talk like that."

"Like what?"

"Like a fucking psycho robot."

A month before, she would've laughed after saying this. Her comment is light in nature, one designed to get me to smile, one intended, at least subconsciously, to get my approval. She wants to forgive me. She wants me back in her life. She wants to confide in me. She wants something I had.

It's my turn to talk. "How did you find out?"

"What? Are you retarded? You were there. That kid you grew up with."

I shake my head.

"You're so crazy," she says.

I know she would only come to me when something she perceived as catastrophic occurred. For Talley, this revolved around Derek. I know he cheated. I know she finally discovered this Truth. I know this because she has no one else to run to.

"About Derek," I say. "How did you find out he was cheating?"

"What?"

"I know that's why you're here."

"Fuck him. And fuck you."

"That's fair."

"No shit it's fair. Thanks for your permission, *Dad*. Oh, that's right, your dad's dead, sorry. Suicide. Your mom from cancer. That's right, isn't it?"

"My parents are alive."

"No fucking shit."

"Did you see it?"

"See what?"

"Derek cheating?"

"You don't get to pretend like you give a shit about me. Not after lying straight to my face for a month."

"You knew he was cheating."

"My question is *why*? That's what I can't figure out. Why the hell did you lie to me about being gay? About your parents? Who the fuck does that?"

I make my way halfway across my studio. I lean against the white wall. Talley is losing steam. Her anger is on the verge of turning inward.

"This isn't about me," I say.

"Yes. Yes, it is."

"I wanted you to like me."

"Then compliment me and buy me a drink like a regular human being."

"I'm not regular."

"Understatement of the century."

"I care about you."

"Don't."

"I do."

"If you did, you wouldn't have lied," Talley says.

Nothing could be further from the truth, but I don't say this. I watch the skin connecting her ears loosen now.

"Did you see him at his practice space with another girl?"

Talley reaches into her oversized purse. She takes out a fifth of whiskey and takes a long pull. It seems like she's playing a part from a movie more than actually blotting out reality.

"You're all the same," she finally says.

"Everyone is the same."

"Men. Men are all the fucking same."

"We're dishonest creatures."

"But I don't cheat. I don't lie. So what the fuck? Why do I get shit on?"

"We seek relationships that reinforce our views of ourselves."

"So this is my fault?"

"Everything is our fault when we live in search of false comforts."

Talley tilts her head. It's pity on her face. I would rather have anger. I lower myself to the wooden floor.

She says, "Do you have any idea of the shit that comes out of your mouth? Or is it so deeply ingrained that it's all automatic?"

"Both."

"Are you really Thirty-Seven?"

"Yes."

"Did you kill…"

"No."

"How can I believe a single thing you say?"

"Through sickness."

"The hell does that even mean?"

"Sickness bears Honesty."

"Right. And Honesty bears change. I read the book."

"I lived the book."

Talley suddenly looks exhausted or maybe just drunk. She sits on my bed. She takes another drink from her bottle. Her red panties show between her oblivious legs.

"How do I know?" Talley says.

"That I'm telling the Truth?"

"Yeah."

"The whites of a person's eyes never lie."

"Psycho."

"That's how you know."

"How?"

I get up. I kneel in front of Talley. I raise my hand and she flinches and this makes me sad. I hold the back of her head. I press my forehead to hers. I tell her to ask me anything, and look at the whites of my eyes. She asks what she's looking for and I tell her Truth.

"Were you part of The Survivors?"

"Yes."

"Have you had sex with men?"

"Yes."

"Were you following me these past few weeks?"

"No."

"Were you following Derek?"

"No."

"Did you really spend three years in jail?"

"Thirty months, most of it in Colorado Mental Health Institute in Pueblo."

"How did you know exactly how Derek cheated?"

"Because I know how people work."

"Do you believe everything Dr. Sick taught you?"

"No."

"Were you happier then?"

"Yes."

"What happened that was so bad that made you run away from home?"

"My mother walked in on my father pleasuring himself at the foot of my bed."

"Jesus Christ," Talley says. She leans back. I want to hold her hands. She blinks a few times in rapid succession. We don't say anything for a while and eye contact feels weird and then she drinks and hands the bottle to me. It burns in a false way. I lean back and sit cross-legged. Talley tilts her head. I tell her she's beautiful. She almost smiles. Then she does, laughing a little. "I walked in to see Derek getting blown by some groupie slut. He was kissing another one."

"I'm sorry."

"But it doesn't matter, right? Like I'm sitting here feeling so sorry for myself when you just told me your father was some sick pedo. That you joined the most infamous cult in recent history. That you spent your youth locked up. Yet I'm the bitch who's crying."

"You don't know any other way. Nobody does. We're taught victimhood is sainthood in its infancy. Our cultural icon is a man nailed to a cross. We are the stars to our own tragedies."

"But you're different."

"I am steeped in wants and fears and selfish bouts of pity."

"Was it like the book?"

"Some of it."

"Do you ever miss it?"

"Every day."

"You could be famous. Rich and shit."

"It's an option."

"I'm so fucking sad," Talley says.

"It will pass."

"It won't. Not the kind I'm talking about."

"You're searching."

"For what?"

"Truth."

"Fuck that. I want to be happy. I want to find a guy who can keep his dick inside of his pants."

I smile. So does Talley. I move onto the bed. We lean against the wall. Our anklebones touch. We pass the bottle between ourselves.

"Sorry I cussed you out," Talley says.

"I deserved it."

"Thought you said self-pity was bad," Talley says.

I smile. "See? I fall victim to the same things."

"I missed you."

"I missed you too."

"And I hate steaming clothes at the store."

"I'd be happy to come back."

"Who offered you the job?"

I laugh.

Talley says, "But I guess if you're desperate…"

"Down to my final two-liter of Mr. Pibb."

"Shit's foul."

"Nectar of the Gods."

Talley puts her arm through mine. She leans her head against my shoulder. She says, "Can you do me a solid?"

"Anything."

"Can you at least pretend to be gay for a little bit longer?"

"Sure."

"No, just don't try to…"

"I won't."

"Promise?"

"Promise."

I wrap my arm around Talley and bring her to my chest and her wig smells different than her hair and I breathe both of them in.

"Mason?"

"Yeah?"

"Can you teach me?"

"Teach you what?"

"How to be like you?"

"You don't want to be like me."

"Yes, I do."

"No, you don't."

"How not to hurt?"

"I hurt."

"How not to care?"

"I care."

"How to be happy?"

"I'm not happy."

Talley's quiet. I feel wetness against my chest and know it's her drool.

"When we did that thing speaking into the ear, that was...you said it was a fraction of what it felt like living in Honesty."

"Smaller than a fraction."

"That was the best I have ever felt," Talley says.

"I know."

"So teach me."

"I'm not One."

"Yes, you are. You're One and I'm Two."

I laugh because I'm uncomfortable. Talley finally joins in. She tells me she drooled all over my shirt. I tell her I already knew that. Her wig is a touch askew and I slip my fingers underneath and her own hair is matted and wet and I place the wig on the floor.

"Would you totally hate me if I passed the fuck out in your bed?" Talley says.

"No, I'll sleep on the floor."

"Don't be *that* gay."

I lay against the wall. I wrap my arm around Talley's stomach. She pushes back against me. She tells me to ignore anything that sounds like a snore. I close my eyes. I match my breath to hers. She says, "Goodnight, One."

I know it's wrong to even joke about it.

I know some jokes cease being funny the moment they are acknowledged.

I know there was only one Dr. James Shepard and I know things got out of hand and I know accidents happened and people searched for anything that would give their death meaning and I know that my objections to Henry O'Connor's book are because it's more true than not and I wonder if Talley had seen a difference in the whites of my eyes during any of my responses and I wonder if Thirty-Eight's tooth I had filed to nothing is now part of something living and then I think about change taking time and Honesty being a journey and then about there being no accidents ever, at least not among those searching for something to keep them from running a blade across their wrists.

"Goodnight, Two."

# 19. SHAVEN

I get back into a routine and it feels good and the holidays approach. I'm at Talley's Tatters four days a week and sometimes even more because I like hanging out. Talley sleeps over most nights. We watch TV on my computer. Sometimes we listen to music. We joke about our hanging out being some sort of training. Sometimes she calls me *sensei*. Sometimes she calls me teacher. Sometimes she calls me *One*.

It's all in good fun, our reading passages out loud from *Dr. Sick*. Talley pokes fun at my platitudes. She makes up her own—*everything is Mr. Pibb; those who seek are impervious to traffic laws; the only Truth is the smear of mascara on your pillow*—and we laugh, hold hands and feel better than the rest of the world. We cannibalize my experience for giggles.

We start to do this more and more.

Jokes cease being jokes when they are acknowledged.

Most desires are initially portrayed as jokes; we gauge reactions by the tautness of one's skin connecting his ears.

Talley still talks about Derek. She talks about wanting to find a guy who's down-to-earth but sexy as hell, and, of course, loyal. This is her way of gauging my reaction. Sometimes I think about sleeping with her. Sometimes I wonder if it'd make things weird like it had with Jerome. Sometimes I don't care.

She's a nonstop series of questions, always in triplets: *What did chemo feel like? Where did you get the drugs? Did you ever think you were going to die?* I try to be Honest. Sometimes she doesn't believe me and presses her forehead to mine and she'll ask the same question and sometimes I change my answer.

One afternoon, she tells me she has a treat for me. She tells me to pack an overnight bag. We get in her Jetta. We drive west. We pass Red Rocks and then we pass Vail and I know where we are going but I play dumb because it's easier. This is the tactic we both employ, denial. We're just friends having fun. Our attitudes are *we're just bored and sick of the bullshit of young adulthood and we're in search of something with meaning but not really it's all for fun we're just so whimsical.*

We get off at the exit for Glenwood Springs. We drive through a touristy town full of old hippies and young kids who want to be hippies. We drive another thirty minutes up the canyon and then we are in Marble with its single street. My breathing is shorter. There's no oxygen in the car. I open the window. I feel sick. I wonder if it's nerves or proximity.

Talley takes a dirt road. We stop in front of the charred remnants of One's home.

I don't say anything as I step out of the car. Talley calls out to me but I'm not listening. I walk to the rubble. Most of it has been cleared, but the foundation is still there, same with some of the larger cedar logs. I remember pressing my face to the glass and seeing Five hold a dying man. I remember knocking and One answering and him welcoming me to the rest of my life.

Talley puts her arm on my back. I turn. I'm crying. I feel something close to regret or maybe it's hatred.

"Oh my God, what's wrong?" she says.

"What are you doing?"

"I thought..."

"What. What did you think?"

"I'm sorry."

"No, you're not."

"Mason, here, let's go. This was a mistake."

Talley takes hold of my hand. I shake loose of her grasp. She's a stupid girl who doesn't know what she was trying to unearth. Her game of pretend had been real for my family; it was still real for me.

"Why?" I say.

"Mason, honey, this was supposed to be fun. But I—"

"Thought only of yourself."

"I'm sorry."

"You thought I'd want to come back here? Why would I want to come back here?"

"You said it was the happiest time of your life."

"And it's gone."

Talley doesn't know what to say to that. My reaction has freaked her out and maybe it's freaked me out too. My whole body trembles.

Talley whispers, "This was a stupid mistake."

"A mistake is a lazy way of shirking blame for selfish actions."

"You're right."

I think about One and Five and Thirty-Eight. I try to feel their presence, but can't. My eyes water. The air smells like sickness and Truth. I remember my first conversation with One standing in this very spot. He'd told me there were no such things as accidents. Talley believes this trip to have been an accident. But it's not an accident. We were supposed to have come here, because at the root of every-thing, we seek a life of Honesty. We clamor for Truth. We found one another. We became as vulnerable as any two who aren't sick possibly can. It's no accident she brought me here. It's no accident she keeps begging me to teach her. It'd been no accident that I'd been fifteen and a minor. It's no accident I am free in the world while the rest of my family are locked up or dead.

I reach out and take Talley's hand.

She's cautious with her smile.

I walk back to her car. I tell her to get her overnight bag. She does. We walk hand in hand around the burned house. We start on a footpath. We don't talk. Talley's hand sweats. We climb in elevation. The sun is being bludgeoned by the peak across the valley. I help her up the boulder. We stand and stare across my home. Talley holds my hand tighter as she peers over the edge.

I tell her to sit down.

She gives a hesitant grin, then does as instructed. I open her leather duffle bag. I find her pink dopp kit. I take out her purple razor.

"What? You just really need a shave right now?"

I hold the razor in my hand. I imagine One holding a rock. I imagine Talley as Thirty-Eight.

"I will ask you a series of questions, and you need to be as Honest as you possibly can, understood?"

"Dude, you're kind of freaking me out," Talley says. Her smile fades when she sees I'm serious.

I say, "Do you want to die?"

Talley stares up at me. She tells me *no*.

"Do you want to leave?"

"No."

"Do you want to live an Honest life amongst a loving family of your own choosing?"

"Yes."

I remove her shoulder-length, dirty-blond wig. Her short hair is wet enough to shave. I tell her to look across the valley and find beauty. She understands what I am about to do. I tell her I will teach her everything I know. I tell her One's beliefs were once transcendent but became misguided. I tell her I'd come up with thoughts of my own. I tell her I'd learned from the greatest mind of this century. I say that there are no accidents; I'd been spared to meet her. I press the purple Bic to the front of her hairline. She gasps. I run the razor back. I tell her certain things will have to change. She nods. I keep shaving her head. I tell her she is free to leave at any point. She tells me she doesn't want to. I tell her this journey will be harder than anything she could ever imagine. She says she's ready. Her scalp is bonewhite. She cries. She asks if she'll find happiness. I tell her happiness is the wrong word, one with a selfish connotation in our current society. I tell her she'll find fulfillment. She reaches around and clasps my left leg. She squeezes. I tell her we all showed up without an invitation, but that didn't mean we weren't invited. Half of her head is bald. A trickle of blood runs toward her left ear from where I'd cut open a mole. I tell her she will soon possess the knowledge of how humans work. This understanding will become ingrained in her. It will sometimes feel like a curse to see motivations so clearly. She says she's ready. I tell her this knowledge will one day cause her to turn against me. She says she'll never betray me. I shave the rest of her head. I tell her it's not about betrayal; the student eventually outlearns the teacher. I tell her everyone succumbs to Self, no matter how hard they try to live in Honesty. She tells me I am different than the previous One. I tell her nobody is different.

I finish.

Talley runs her hand over her bald head. She stands. She's ecstatic. She presses her head to mine. I love the feeling of baldness

underneath my fingertips. I sit on the boulder. I hand her the razor. She says she doesn't want to cut me and I tell her cuts don't
matter. She shaves my head. The mountain air greets my bare skin,
a welcome feeling, Thanksgiving dinners and returned phone
calls and a father's drunken steps climbing up the stairs while he
believed you to be asleep.

Soon, I am bald.

Talley is bald.

We sit on a boulder.

The initial gifts of shedding oneself are evident in our mutual
feelings of tranquility.

"Now what?" Talley asks.

"We become sick."

# 20. SICK (I)

Ipecac is cheap and leaves your teeth feeling acid-burnt and forces you to hover over paint buckets purchased at Home Depot for ninety-nine cents. It's as close as we can get to Cytoxan. I haven't vomited in close to three years and it's more violent than I remember, or maybe it's just the difference of catalyzing agents. We sit in my bathroom. Two looks beautiful with her head shaved. She rests her cheek on the toilet seat. I have my elbows propped against the orange bucket. We've expelled everything inside of us. She asks if we are done. I say, "Again."

# 21. GIFT OF UNDERSTANDING

I was chosen to be part of a nuclear family, the Johnsons from Durango. We had fake passports and wigs made of real hair, a rented Suburban, and went on a family vacation over winter break. One was my father; Five was my mother. She looked pretty with raven-black hair and One looked handsome with his salt-and-pepper curls and I felt silly in my pompadour poof. We were to drive to Tijuana to procure more Cytoxan. It was to be simple, a treat really.

We spent the night in Las Vegas. My eyes hurt from the strobes of neon. The scads of people freighted me. I'd never been to Vegas. It had an energy, a pulsating red that was alluring. We stayed at the MGM Grand. I wasn't sure why we chose to stay at a fancy place on the Strip, but then One and Five said they were going out to gamble as not to raise suspicion, and I understood this was a form of Reprieve for them. I watched a movie on HBO about a cop whose family was murdered. I thought about pleasuring myself during a sex scene but felt embarrassed for some reason.

Two hours passed.

I started to worry. We didn't have phones. There was no way I could get ahold of One or Five, save for going to the front desk and asking for a page over the PA. But One would be angry with the drawing of attention. He'd tell me it was my selfish fear of abandonment that caused all eyes to turn on our family.

I watched a sitcom my father had loved. I wondered if he was watching the same thing. I wanted to feel connected to him. I wondered if they still were together. Probably. I'm sure he made something up or maybe he denied the whole thing, wouldn't talk about it, refused to acknowledge what my mother had walked in on, so that night became anonymous like all the others, their minds shifting to the possible reasons I may have run away.

Three hours.

I thought about police having recognized One. I thought about the two of them tied up in some forgotten cellar being beaten with phone books. I told myself I was being stupid and they were probably having fun and then I felt immature because I was almost sixteen and hadn't stepped foot off of One's property in over five months, and here I was in Vegas for the first time in my life.

I took the room key and headed to the elevator. This was the first time I had disobeyed One. I walked through the casino. Everyone smoked and drank and was fat. Nobody looked happy, not even the high rollers with pretty women on their arms. I made my way outside. People shuffled down the streets as if on invisible conveyer belts. Everyone looked out of place. A black woman in five-inch heels handed me her card with her exposed breasts on the front and she told me I was cute as hell, she'd cut her rate in half, and I smiled because I'd never spoken with a hooker. I watched a grouping of college-aged pricks try to pick up some Midwestern housewives. The women laughed and then touched the gym-constructed shoulders of the kids and then they left as a group. A homeless man in a wheelchair rolled by, a Puerto Rican flag taped to his armrest. He'd written *LIAR* in black Sharpie across the flag's fabric.

I leaned against the wall and then I crouched. I felt homeless. I felt invisible. People came here looking for something that wasn't real. Or maybe it all was real and their lives in Ohio weren't. A man in a button-down short-sleeved shirt approached me. His thinning hair was combed at a severe rightward angle. He asked if I was okay. I nodded. He asked if I was alone. I told him I was meeting people. He asked if I had repented in time for the Rapture. It was in this moment when I received my first Gift of Understanding. One had told me about these moments. He said it was a natural byproduct of living in Honesty. He said the world's falsities would fall off like so many rusted shackles. Insights would initially come as a strengthened gut reaction, but would, over time and hard work and the destruction of Self, arrive with brilliant flashes of color, a still photograph or a short montage of movie clips that depicted a person's true motivations. He said this gift would set me apart from my fellows. He said it was a trait that the rest of the world would call psychic because it was easier for them to believe in the supernatural and occult than to believe somebody could be that in harmony with Truth.

My first Gift of Understanding arrived like an exploded light bulb. I saw this evangelical's apartment, everything brown but getting lighter as the sun shone through drawn blinds. I saw a peanut butter and jelly sandwich with a bite missing next to a half-drunk glass of lemonade. And then I saw myself in a brown recliner with worn armrests. I saw myself with fluttering eyes, me eventually losing the fight, my eyes closing, my mouth ajar. I saw this man's smile as he snapped his fingers in front of my face. I felt his trembling hands against my waist as he fumbled with my buckle. And then I saw him commit acts my father only fantasied about.

I looked up at the man standing above me in the dry Vegas night. I told him I wasn't interested.

"You're not interested in Eternal Salvation?"

"I'm not interested in going to your disgusting apartment and being drugged through a sandwich and lemonade and being raped repeatedly."

The man's face went from feigned care to utter shock. He wanted to protest but couldn't. He stepped backward. He stared at me and then turned and walked double-time in the opposite direction and he didn't look back even once.

I straightened up.

I'd been given a Gift of Understanding. It'd been amazing, ethereal, God-like. But more importantly, it meant I was doing the work in earnest. It meant I was firmly rooted in the Path of Honesty. It meant I was glimpsing small Truths.

I headed back to the MGM.

I was half a block away when I saw One and Five. It took a second to recognize them with the wigs and clothes bought at Walmart. They didn't see me. I merged to my right so I was surrounded by taller people. One and Five held hands and they laughed and they stumbled and I realized they were drunk and were in love. I talked myself out of them being in love through a series of rationalizations I could almost believe. They looked happy. They looked like everyone else. Five fell over. One couldn't stop laughing. This felt like betrayal and like middle school and like an accident, both on their part, and on my behalf as a witness. There were no accidents. A homeless man with *LIAR* scribbled across a Puerto Rican Flag. A preacher pedophile. A glimpse of One and Five being drunken idiots.

I made my way back up to the room.

I felt alone and bad about everything.

I told myself they were granting themselves Reprieve in a different form. I told myself we were a loving family of our own choosing. I told myself everyone faltered, that it was our nature.

I told myself I was on a path to being granted the Gifts of Truth. I told myself every religion aimed at this same Holy Grail. I told myself nobody had ever found it. I told myself I was close or at least headed in the right direction.

One and Five were hungover the next morning. The car ride was quiet. Alcohol sweated through their skin. We drove across Southern California. We approached the border. One went over our story: we were Douglass, Rebecca, and Timothy Johnson; we were from Durango, Colorado. Douglass was in oil and gas, Rebecca was in elementary education, and Timothy excelled in theater. We were vacationing for winter break in San Diego, and they wanted to show the boy some culture, so they decided to take a day trip to Mexico.

I understood small falsities were necessary when searching for larger Truths.

The line wasn't that long because evidently nobody gave a shit who went into Mexico. One handed over our passports and the border patrol looked at them and then us and when he peered in the window to see me, I felt like an imposter and I smiled. He waved us through.

Every mile, things became less familiar. There were so many people. Men wore cowboy boots. Things were bleached by the sun. I smelled the ocean and I smelled diesel gas. Traffic was bad. We inched along. One looked nervous, which I'd never seen. Tourists stuck out like flashing beacons. We parked in a lot. One paid a man and then gave him extra to look after the car. We got out.

One told us we had to kill a couple of hours. We walked down a section of the city that was a little nicer with trashcans that didn't overflow. We made our way to the beach. Kids played soccer and older kids played volleyball and a fat woman in a red shirt walked around selling burritos and bottles of water. Five told me to take off my shoes. I did. We both rolled up our jeans. One told us he'd watch our stuff. Five took my hand and we walked across the sand and it felt good between my toes. The water looked too dark. I thought about pollution and then I thought about being in Mexico to buy Cytoxan and realized it didn't matter. A small wave washed against my ankles.

"Sorry again about last night," Five said.

"Stop," I said. "I was asleep by ten. Had no idea you guys were even still out."

Five let go of my head. She brought her index finger to my face. She rubbed just inside of my ear. She said, "This."

"Huh?"

"This part of the body has a hell of a time being dishonest."

"What do you mean?"

"I mean the jaw is the scapegoat of a person's tension. It is the last to be instructed to lower its guard."

"Like a tell?"

"Exactly."

"Just for lying?"

"For everything. You need to watch for changes in tension. It can tell more than the whites of eyes."

"Oh."

"Likewise, if you're ever in a situation where dishonesty is needed to serve Truth, the first thing you need to do is separate your jaw, still with your mouth closed. Then bring your teeth to-gether, but gently, so they are barely touching."

"Okay."

Five took her hand off my face but still looked at me. I squinted because the sun was her halo. She said, "So, once again, I'm sorry about last night."

"That's okay."

"Were you worried?"

"Yes."

"That was selfish of us."

"Are you two in love?"

Five took my hand. We started walking along the edge of the surf. When she didn't respond for a few seconds, I looked over. I noticed then that the front of her jaw jutted forward ever so slightly, then retracted. The skin connecting her ear was loose. I realized she'd just unclenched her jaw and realigned her teeth, as she'd instructed me to do. She glanced down with a smile. She said, "No, at least no more than I'm in love with all the rest of you."

We went to two different pharmacies, buying the maximum amount of Cytoxan allowed in each. One hid the white rectangular boxes inside of a rolling suitcase. I wanted to tell him this wasn't a very good hiding spot but he didn't seem to worry and neither did Five and then it was time to head back to California. The border took forever going the other direction. Mexicans sold cheap souvenirs between our idling cars. Dogs walked around on taut leashes sniffing for drugs or bombs or maybe people. We inched forward. We had passports and a narrative for being in Mexico.

After an hour, we were about to speak with the US Customs Agents. Except they weren't like normal agents because they had machine guns strapped across their chests. I felt ill. Five's neck sweated. One spoke to me, his eyes meeting mine through the rearview mirror: "We don't talk. Nobody living in Honesty says a word."

He rolled down the window with a big fake smile plastered on his face. He handed over our passports. The patrolman checked our names and then our faces. He asked our reason for being in Mexico. I watched the skin connecting One's ear and it was the same as Five—jaw forward, realigning of teeth, then response—and he told them to get some culture and the man didn't smile even though we all did.

I watched the border patrolman. He sensed something wasn't right. He sensed he was being lied to. And it made sense because he faced this a thousand times a day, people presenting their best selves in order to gain admittance to what he guarded, people lying, people engaged in every form of deceit. But he didn't understand what, exactly, he was searching for. He had intuition but not enough to motion us to pull over to be searched. Because we knew something he didn't: we knew how people worked.

He waved us through.

I understood we navigated the world with something close to a superpower. I understood this was a gift from the work we were doing. I understood that One had nearly blown it, not because the patrolman had the same powers as us, but because One's weren't as strong as they needed to be. He was slacking. He was letting Self creep back into his life—Five, too. They were faltering. I pushed this thought aside, as was my habit. But I let it come back. I let it come back because it was Truth, and that, above all else—any person or group or loving family of my own choosing—was what I served.

# 22. SICK (II)

Monday through Wednesday we take stool softeners and laxatives. We are at Talley's Tatters sitting behind the counter and we don't listen to the music or pretend to work, just hold our stomachs, our bodies chambers of constriction. We sweat. We take turns in the bathroom. At first we're embarrassed about our smells. One afternoon, Two can't hold it while I'm in the restroom and then I hear her whimper and I know she's had an accident. There are no accidents. I help change her clothes. I use wet paper towels to clean her legs. She stops crying as I clean her. She doesn't make any self-deprecating comments because we are past that.

# 23. FEAR

Fifteen got some sort of infection and it moved from his sinuses to his lungs in no time. His breathing was like dragged metal chains. He died by the next morning.

I was chosen to pry a tooth from his mouth.

We buried him next to Thirty-Eight.

I took a second Reprieve because it was offered.

Snow fell.

Christmas arrived. We listened to an Elvis record where he sang holiday classics. One gave us a treat: Mr. Pibb. The carbonation burned the insides of my ears and the sugar attacked my enamel-less teeth. We ate our rice and things were good with the lights turned low. We took turns saying one thing we were grateful for. We all said one another.

One stood. He made sure to make eyes at each and every one of us. He told us that he'd originally planned on waiting until the summer solstice to discuss this matter, but knew in his heart that the time was right.

I shifted my weight. Five's elbow dug into my ribs and I liked this feeling. One stood in his black scrubs. His eyes were sunken but bright. He said, "As a whole, our level of Honesty is higher than it has ever been. This is good. This is the purpose of our lives. Or rather, it *has been* the purpose of our lives here thus far. But as you all know, Honesty is only the first step."

Some of us smiled.

"Sickness bears Honesty; Honesty bears change."

We agreed.

"But what change have we accomplished?"

Our smiles faded.

"We have created a loving family of our own choosing. We could continue with what we are doing, and this would be fine. We could continue believing we are following the Path, that we are in communion with Truth. But to what avail? What good would this do a single person, other than ourselves? And if we serve no other people, then isn't all of this work a way of bolstering our own selfish ends?"

Three started to say something, but One shot him a look, and then Three was quiet.

"We are vessels of Honesty. We are disciples of Truth. We need to enact change."

One paced around the living room. All of us looked up at him and some of us were starting to understand this was a call to arms of sorts, something we needed, something we'd been waiting for without even realizing it.

"Tonight, we will take Reprieve. But we will do it alone. Each of you will find a solitary place outside to take your Reprieve, which will be double the amount normally ingested. You must force yourself against the outer limits of the safe enclosure we've created. You need to meditate upon this question: How does each one of you, personally, enact change upon the greater world?"

We split up.

I walked outside and up the path. One by one, we dropped off from the group. I kept walking. Snow filled my shoes. I walked to the base of the cliff. I sat in the snow. I shivered and told myself to quit being weak. I poured the DMT onto the foil. I told myself I was living in Honesty because I'd been given a Gift of Understanding and had completed two rounds of chemo and because I felt ready to breach our bubble and force others against Truth.

I took Reprieve.

Things got real dark. I understood I was alone. Not just in the present, but always. This wasn't a bad feeling; it merely *was*. I navigated my way through every conceivable shade of red of my mind's eye. And then my vision cleared a bit, shapes taking form, a middle-aged woman with the trappings of the wealthy walking a Shih Tzu. This woman loved the dog. It was all she had, this dog a stand-in for family and for God and for a reason to keep on living. I envisioned the dog breaking free from the leash. I imagined it running into a street. I saw the dog vanish underneath the hood of a truck. I didn't see the woman's face, but I knew she'd just experienced a loss that would shatter her world. I knew this was a form of suffering she'd never even allowed herself to fathom. I knew the root of sickness is suffering. I knew the death of her dog was a gift, a catalyst for her to start a journey toward Honesty.

I talked with One later that night. I told him what I'd seen. He put his hand on the back of my head. He pressed his forehead to mine. He didn't need to say anything. I knew I had made him proud.

Seven of us were chosen to carry out the plans to enact change. We were forbidden to speak of them with anyone else. The following morning, we packed inside of One's Jeep. He drove us to the Greyhound station in Glenwood Springs. I expected all of us to get out, but it was only me. He told me to get a ticket to Golden and carry out my plan and then get a ticket back. He gave me three hundred dollars. I didn't want to be alone. The others said they loved me. I believed them.

I wore my civilian clothes, the ones I'd shown up in. The jeans were four inches too big around the waist. The bus was half full and I rested my head against the window and the vibrations made me sleepy. Across the aisle, a little girl played with her mother's phone. She smiled at me and her teeth were a mess, but I thought she was cute and I hoped she'd have a good life.

I fell asleep.

I awoke when we stopped moving.

I asked the little girl's mom where we were and she told me Golden and I thanked her and got off the bus. It was dusk. My coat wasn't warm enough. I stood in the Walmart parking. Part of me wanted to go inside and get gloves, but that seemed selfish. I headed up the hill, away from the quaint and artificial downtown. Rows of subdivisions stuck out against a hill that might have been a mountain.

One hadn't really given me instructions. He'd listened to my vision and told me to enact it. He said Honesty would guide me. He told me I'd know what to do.

I walked about a half mile. I turned down a residential street. They had lamps, so I kept walking. Every house was mostly dark except for a bottom room with the epileptic flashing of television sets. I kept my hands in my jacket pockets. I ran my right hand over the plastic handle of the knife.

I turned twice more—once left, once right.

The houses were nice but maybe not as nice as they'd been before.

There weren't street lamps.

I stopped in front of a house with Christmas decorations. An inflatable Frosty waved in the breeze. Red and blue and green lights dangled from the porch ceiling. An actual snowman stood next to

Frosty. There were two plastic sleds next to the front door. I noticed some of the trampled snow was discolored.

It was here where I was given my second Gift of Understanding.

Like my first, it came with a sudden flash of a three-second movie clip: a family of four, a family ascending in tax brackets, a family who went to church and felt blessed with having a son before a daughter, a family who cherished the ritualization of the seasons and of the day and of bath time and story time and Eskimo kisses. It was a family who hadn't been forced to question a single thing in their lives. Nothing. Hard work and God granting them their entitled slice of America.

But it wasn't enough.

I knew this; I'd lived this.

I knew the wife was already getting bored. I knew something nagged inside of her, told her she could've done more, and this feeling had attached itself to buying more accessories for her house, cemented itself in the notion of needing her children to be better than the others at their all-Caucasian elementary school. It would be affairs before long. The same with the husband. His itch would take the form of weeklong *guys' trips* where other cuckolded dads would pretend they were blue collar and single and happy. The kids: they didn't have a chance. They'd grow up seeing life as a checklist, one that needed to be completed but bore no fruit. They would follow a damned path because they believed themselves without options.

The family, as a whole, was entombed in Self.

They lived their entire existence based on first loves, favorite memories, and biggest regrets.

Every single action they took was meant to fortify them from suffering, from Truth.

The walkway was shoveled. I headed around the side of the house. I thought about traceable footprints but not really. I was a ghost to these people. The backyard was smaller and unused. I understood this was because it was where the dog went to the bathroom. I avoided mounds of brown. I walked to the back door. A black square covered the bottom third of the door. I walked along the edge of the two stairs so as to not make them creak. I felt like my father walking to my room. I knelt. I pulled the doggy door back with the tip of my buck knife. A gush of warm air blew past the heavy plastic flap. The opening was big, but not big enough for a dog I had to worry about.

I was giving them a gift.

I was enacting change.

I bit down on the blade. I put my left arm through the opening, then my head, then my right. The only light on inside came from the plugged-in appliances. My ribs pressed against the opening. I was quiet. I kept pulling and then my torso lay against their wooden floor. I turned over onto my back, careful as I slid my legs through the doggy door.

That was when I heard the pattering of nails.

I reached into my pocket and pulled out a half-eaten package of Nutter Butters I'd purchased at the Greyhound station. I positioned myself on my knees. A white poodle rounded the corner of the kitchen island. It barked once upon seeing me. I was all smiles and whispered placations, my left hand outstretched, my treat an offering. The poodle stared. It sniffed. Its manicured tail wagged. This dog was the same as the family, it had been conditioned to be oblivious to threats. Its nose was cold against my palm. It ate the cookies. I petted its curly hair. I ran fingers behind its floppy ears. It licked the floor for remnants of peanut butter. I needed to act and it needed to be now and it was the right thing because it served the greater good of humanity, but also these people, and my body tingled and there were no accidents and I thought of how pleased

One had been when I'd shared my plan and I brought my right hand to my mouth and took hold of the knife's handle and the dog licked my arm and I took hold of the scruff of its neck and pulled its head back and saw the soft spot underneath its jaw and brought the blade to its throat and thought of seeing One and Five drunk in Las Vegas and how this wasn't Honest and then about Five lying to me as we walked in the ocean and something deep inside of me told me change could be enacted without the finality of death.

I stood.

The poodle walked with me over to the refrigerator.

They had a magnetized to-do list with a golf pencil attached to it.

I pulled the list down and walked to the island. I petted the dog. I wrote: *I could have killed every single one of you. You can't fortify yourselves from* TRUTH. *Reading this note is my gift to you.*

I left the note on the granite countertop. I walked back to the door. I thought about opening it, but worried about an alarm. I crouched down and pushed the rubber flap. The dog barked. I spun around and told him he was a good boy and to be quiet. He barked again, three shrill yelps. I grabbed hold of his snout. I squeezed and told him *no*. He whimpered. I let go. He was quiet. But when I crouched back down, he barked once more, and in that instant, I acted without thinking, grabbing the scruff of his neck, lifting him off the floor. I undid the deadbolt and opened the door. There was no alarm, at least nothing audible. I shut the door and carried the dog across the backyard and into an alley. He whimpered. I set him down, still holding onto his neck. I undid my belt and wrapped it through his collar. Lights turned on in the house I'd just been in. I ran the dog down the alley. I looked back. The kitchen lights turned on. I knew the husband was searching for his dog. I knew he was now coming across the note I'd written. I knew his entire sense of the world had been demolished. I knew he was being forced up against the Truth that promotions and Christmas cards and weekend trips to the mountains weren't enough to keep bad things at bay.

I let the dog go without its collar a mile from the house and bought a Greyhound ticket to Glenwood Springs that left at seven in the morning. I found a truck stop diner and ordered toast and a Mr. Pibb. A few truckers eyed me like my father had when he walked into my room, pretending he hadn't known I was changing. I kept my eyes down. I worked my nail file against Thirty-Eight's and Fifteen's teeth, alternating every five minutes. I debated if I should tell One what I'd really done or lie about having killed a dog. I wondered if he'd be able to tell if I were being Honest. I'd come too far to start engaging in selfish forms of communication. There were no accidents. I'd written that note for a reason, a reason I couldn't quite understand, but maybe didn't need to understand.

But that was bullshit.

I understood exactly why I'd written the note: fear breeds sickness.

One had never said this, but it was the operational Truth everything else he taught stemmed from.

Therefore, fear bears change.

And I'd just given the world something to fear.

# 24. SICK (III)

Two's having trouble swallowing. She grimaces every few seconds. At night, she doesn't bother trying to shield me from this sight, letting her saliva soak my pillows. I ask to see the inside of her throat. She opens her mouth. Her breath is a sour I know well. Her throat is angry and swollen with a pristine coating of freshly fallen snow around her tonsils. I tell her she needs to see a doctor and she tells me she's fine.

Two days later, I see her holding her throat as she swallows. It's like she's trying to make her esophagus larger by pulling her skin outward. I tell her enough is enough and she puts up a small protest but I insist.

She goes to urgent care.

She comes back five hours later with antibiotics and painkillers and some sort of numbing agent she's to drink. She tells me she's burnt all of the tender lining of her throat. The burns have become infected. She says the doctor gave her a lecture about bulimia.

Two won't stop with her doses of ipecac.

I make sure she at least takes the antibiotics after she's swallowed and expelled the poison.

# 25. THE NOTES

One wasn't upset about the changing of my plan. He wasn't mad I hadn't killed the dog. He kept asking what I'd written. I told him again and again. He mulled over these words. The skin connecting his ear wasn't tight but wasn't loose either.

That night, One gathered all of us downstairs.

He said that those of us who'd enacted change had done very well. He said change had to start somewhere. He said people were living different lives than they were twenty-four hours before. Then One looked at me. He winked. He said, "An ingenious idea has been brought to my attention. This will further our goal while minimizing any potential risk. We will utterly shake the foundation of this nation's false sense of security. It will be called The Notes."

One bought a laptop in Glenwood Springs. He didn't pay for Internet at the house, but he'd go into town and sit at the coffee shop to use their Wi-Fi. He said he needed to keep tabs on our progress. This seemed reasonable.

He'd come back to the house where we waited. He'd tell us about a small town in Idaho where a note showed up. He'd tell us a wife being interviewed in Spokane cried hysterically, told the reporter and the world that nobody was safe. A death threat in Madison, Wisconsin. Helena, Montana. Salt Lake City, Utah.

After a month, CNN ran a ninety-second story about a series of ominous notes left in homes across the western United States. They showed one note from Lawrence, Kansas. I wasn't sure whose handwriting it was. It read, "*I could have killed every single one of you. You can't fortify yourselves from _TRUTH_. Reading this note is my gift to you.*" They speculated about the culprits, the causes, the probability of this being some sort of viral Internet hoax. They showed one family in Reno who sat on a couch, each of them touching some part of another. The father said, "It [the note] made us realize how precious life really is. In a strange way, it brought us closer together."

The farthest east we went was Toledo. The farthest south was El Paso. We wrote fifty-six notes. Most of us just wrote one, but those traveling long distances sometimes did two. One forbade me to take another trip. He told me I had done my part. He told me it was of more importance to focus on a rededication to sickness so as to stave off any grandiosity that may arrive from enacting change on such a large scale.

I agreed.

I started a new cycle of chemo.

I cried into a plastic paint bucket.

But it was different this time; the sicker I became, the closer to Honesty I felt. I was greedy to experience paralyzing pain because I knew the rewards awaiting me.[7]

---

7 Henry O'Connor obviously has a chapter on *The Notes*. But the chapter doesn't really get the essence of what the notes were meant to accomplish. Instead, O'Connor focuses on their sentiment, the breaking and entering, the dispersal of The Survivors across the country as individual "cells of terrorism"—as a precursor to The Day of Gifts. He writes, "Much like the heroin addict's gateway drug being a loosely rolled joint,

The Notes were The Survivors' initial foray into the world of inflicting terror. They experienced a taste; they wanted more. Fear became their drug of choice. The only cure was an act inspiring greater amounts of it."

Maybe this is true.

Maybe we felt the rush that came from enacting change.

Maybe we understood what it meant to be feared.

I don't know. I really don't.

But I *do* know that The Notes were not merely a stepping stone to The Day of Gifts. They were an end in their own right. They were a tool to shatter the nation's selfish walls of false security. They were meant to cause suffering. They were meant to have people turn toward Honesty. They were meant to accomplish exactly what the family in Reno professed.

# 26. SICK (IV)

Two and I are at Talley's Tatters. It's Wednesday afternoon. We're sick, but not that sick, and we're listening to a collection of Elvis covers. Two isn't wearing a wig, as has become habit.

The door opens.

Derek walks in. He's skinnier than I remember, but not like us. His is a form of his stature, ours a form of sickness. He looks at me and then Two and he does a double take at her bald head and he almost smiles but doesn't.

"Jesus, Talley, are you okay?"

I watch Two. She has become nervous, her energy pulling inward, her right arm crossing her stomach. I know she's thinking about her appearance and about being bald and about the love she'd believed to share with this man, the love she'd conjured in her childhood, the love that looked so much like passion yielding to suburban domestication.

"What are..."

"The hair?" Derek says.

"...you doing here?"

"I came to see..." Derek looks. He steps closer to Two. "Is there somewhere we can talk?"

"*Talk*?" Two says.

"More privately?"

"I don't have anything to say to you."

"Baby, please."

They both turn in my direction. I put up my hands to indicate I understand they want me gone. I get off the stool behind the counter.

"No, you're good," Two says. "Stay."

"Then can we step outside?" Derek says.

"No."

"Baby."

"Not your baby."

"Please."

"Anything you have to say, you can say in front of…Mason."

"Are you two…" Derek looks at Two, then me. I don't turn my gaze, but stare even harder. Derek's mind is sex, like most every other person's. That's how the world makes sense to him. That's how he understands his ex-girlfriend's refusal to speak to him— the only possible cause being another man, not himself, a complete denial of culpability for his actions.

Derek says, "You've got to be kidding me. *Him*? You're fucking *him*?"

"What if I am?" Two says.

"Then you're an even bigger slut than I thought."

Two smiles. She looks down, rubbing her hand over her scalp. She looks back at Derek, still grinning. "You're so fucking pathetic."

Derek reaches forward and touches Two's arm and she recoils and he frowns and says, "I'm sorry. I didn't mean that."

"There are no accidents."

"What? Baby, that's what I came here to talk about. What happened…it *was* an accident. I was drunk and one thing led to another and—"

"I pity you," Two says.

"Can we please just talk in private?"

"Because you're so full of shit and you have no idea."

"I'm sorry."

"The whole *I'm a rock star* thing is so trite. So false. You live in Denver. You play venues where you know the booking agent. You're nothing."

Derek makes another reach for Two's arm. She slaps his hand. It's Derek's turn to laugh, to feign bewilderment. His body language becomes empathetic and he tries one more time. "People are worried. You've completely disappeared. Nobody's seen you. Are you okay? Like health-wise and everything?"

"Never felt better."

"Why don't you come out tonight? No pressure with us or whatever, but just come hang out. Everyone misses you."

"Everyone who hasn't called in over a month?"

"What? Yeah. No. We're worried," he says. "*I'm* worried."

"There are no accidents."

"What are you talking about?"

"I was supposed to see you with those girls."

"I was drunk, baby. Completely wasted. I'm so sorry. You have to believe me."

Two reaches out her hand. She strokes the side of Derek's face. He smiles. She rubs his cheek. She says, "Right here." She moves her hands to Derek's eyes. He closes his lids. He's a born-again awaiting holy water. "And right here." She brings her hand back to her side. Derek opens up his eyes; there's hope there. I understand what she is doing and I love her and am proud like a parent or maybe a little brother.

"Those two places can't lie."

"I'm not—"

"Yes, yes you are. But that's okay. I don't fault you for this. You have no defense against deceit."

"Baby."

Two shakes her head. Derek understands this is a moment of finality. His energy builds. He rubs his nose with the back of his hand. He shakes his head, forces himself to smile.

"This is a mistake," he says. He nods in my direction. "This fucking creep…not your finest moment."

"It was great seeing you," Two says.

"Whenever you're done playing identity crisis with that freak, come find me. No, strike that. You had your chance."

"And what a marvelous chance it was."

Derek laughs. He backs up. He looks at me, trying to intimidate. It isn't working because he feels my gaze lacking selfish fear. He turns back to Two. "Oh, and a quick pro tip: you looking fucking horrible with a shaved head."

"Thanks, babe."

"Crazy," Derek says. "You're fucking crazy."

"Love ya. Thanks for stopping in to visit."

Derek struggles for a departing comment and then falters and shakes his head and walks to the door, slamming it as hard as he can on the way out. Two turns toward me. She smiles and I am out from behind the counter and I take her in my arms and her body shakes and she presses her head to mine and the whites of her eyes are bright and I don't have to tell her I'm proud because she understands and "Blue Moon" plays and things are good.

Two says, "It's time for our noon dose."

# 27. STUDENT

Something changed after The Notes. There was a different energy around the house, an anticipatory excitement. Before there'd be stretches of days when one of us wouldn't say a word. We were sick. We were on a journey inward. We didn't have much to say. But that changed. After The Notes, we talked at all hours of the day. There'd be groups of us huddled around the patio or in the kitchen or even in our dorms, eight of us in a communal conversation, naked in our bunks. We had ideas and we had untrue reports and we had stories of our own adventures across the country. Twenty-One kept talking about how the wife and mother of the house he entered in Santa Barbara had come downstairs to the kitchen while he was writing his message and he'd had to crawl into the pantry for cover, but the woman opened the pantry and stood two feet away eating handfuls of Honey Nut Cheerios—and we listened on with smiles.

We felt like we were changing the world.

We felt better than everyone else.

We felt like we were the only ones who'd ever been privy to Truth.

Something else changed, too. Or maybe I simply became more attuned to what had been going on around me the entire time. One and Five spent more and more time together. I told myself it was nothing out of the ordinary. They'd lived together for over three years; they talked in groups; they were siblings in Honesty. But I couldn't forget Five's lie to me while standing in the ocean. She loved him. And he loved her.

This concept messed me up because it felt unfair to the rest of us. We were a family, and families didn't choose favorites, and why wasn't I either of their favorite? On some level I realized these feelings were nothing but jealousy. I felt unloved and spurned and neglected, even though I was surrounded by people who held me as I got sick. I wanted One's approval. I wanted Five's sexual interest. I wanted One's sexual interest. I wanted Five's approval.

Wants. Selfishness. Fears.

They came on strong and I felt alone with them because One and Five were my usual sounding boards. I asked One for more Cytoxan and he told me I was already pushing the absolute boundary of what my body could handle. I begged. He said it was beautiful, a boy searching with this much Honesty. He told me he'd give me an extra shot a week, but only for a month.

One night, I was especially sick. Everyone in my dorm was asleep and I couldn't stop vomiting and I didn't want to wake them so I curled on the couch and prayed for death and for a different life and for my selfishness to disintegrate once and for all.

That was when I heard a door open and close.

I slipped off the couch and crawled to the hallway.

I saw a silhouette standing at One's closed door. I was pretty sure it was Five. She knocked softly. The door opened. I watched One take hold of Five. I watched them kiss. I watched their bodies press. I watched them disappear behind One's locked door.

I waited in the hallway for close to two hours.

The door finally opened. At first, neither of them saw me. They pressed foreheads. Five turned to head back to the dorm. That's when she saw me. She put her hand to her mouth and said, "Fuck." One turned in his doorway. He stood there completely slack. He was my father after completion. He walked past Five. I feared he was going to hit me. He knelt down to my level. The whites of his eyes shown. He asked if I was well enough to walk to the boulder. I thought about Thirty-Eight going to the boulder with One and then Thirty-Eight falling, the back of his head caved in. One didn't wait for me to respond. He took hold of my arm and forced me to stand. He wrapped the quilt I'd been carrying around my shoulders. He told me to step into any pair of boots.

We didn't say anything on the walk to the boulder. The air was dark but changing, the first hints of light coming from the calls of invisible crows. I thought about being killed and I thought about being betrayed and I thought about the fact we had no rules and they'd done nothing wrong and that some of us fornicated because it was done in Honesty and then I thought about how nobody was allowed in One's room and it was different, what I'd seen first in Vegas and then in the hallway, different because it was exclusive. Different because it was love like the rest of the world. Selfish.

We sat on the boulder. My entire body shivered. One didn't say anything while I got sick. My lungs felt full of fluid. I couldn't remember the last time I'd felt awkward around One.

Finally, he spoke. "Life is funny sometimes."

I didn't say anything. I didn't even look over.

"It's the cruelest creature imaginable, but its patience is astounding." One blew on his bare hands. "It gives you gifts before you know how to handle them. Then it rips those gifts away. If we do the work to humble ourselves—the work we're doing here—then life will once again give you her bountiful goods."

"Do you love her?"

"I love all of you."

"Why are you hiding it?"

One took a second to respond, "Can you feel it?'

"What?"

"How close we are to changing everything? It's happening. We're doing it. *You're* doing it."

"It's dishonest."

"Bringing the world Truth is the opposite."

"Your relationship."

"Is a gift. It's a gift for living in Honesty. It's the world's way of mending past transgressions."

"Why her?"

"Those who seek find one another."

"Why not me?"

"When you are ready, you'll be rewarded with a symbiotic love."

I didn't tell One that that wasn't what I'd meant.

"And it will be like nothing you've ever experienced. Believe me. Because you are searching more diligently than anyone I've ever seen. Including myself. The rewards awaiting you are going to be infinite. Otherworldly. Literally, from another world. You have accessed a level of Truth that most of humanity doesn't even know exists. And you're still so young. It's..." One stopped talking. He shook his head. "Honestly, and this pains my selfish core to admit it, but I will: I'm jealous of you."

I couldn't help but smile.

"I am. I really am. The entire notion of The Notes was your idea."

"I didn't really think of it."

"You did. It arose naturally from within you, because you are so thoroughly plugged into Truth. And when you are in that trance-like harmony, every action is purposeful, every idea is Honest, and everything you do produces change."

One put his arm around my shoulder. I shivered and he rubbed my back and we stared at the world trying to wake up.

"This is a moment in history that will be remembered," One said.

"Right now?"

One laughed. He said, "What we are doing. What *you* are doing." He stopped rubbing my back and then I felt cold. "If I confide in you, will you promise me it doesn't leave this boulder?"

I nodded. I thought about living with secrets. One must've seen the concern because he told me lies of omission were okay if they served Truth. I told him I wouldn't say anything.

"I'm going to need you in the next few months, more so than ever. Not just because we've embarked upon the impossible task of righting the world, but because…"

One trailed off. I finally looked up and over. He stared down at me. His face looked swollen from that angle. I tried to look at the whites of his eyes but his pupils were in the way.

"The true student knows when he's in the presence of his superior."

"I know you're sup—"

"I'm talking about myself."

"Huh?"

"You have a once-in-a-millennium yearning for Truth."

I stared at trees emerging from nothing. My body shook, but it wasn't from the cold and it wasn't from the chemo, but from the power of recognition, *self*-recognition, esteem.

"I have taken this group as far as I can," One said. "My strengths are in the rebuilding of broken lives. Of creating family. Of harvesting love. It is you who will lead the world to change."

I didn't respond.

"I will assist you until you are ready to lead. The others…I think it best if we keep things status quo. We don't mention Five and mine's relationship. We don't mention the proverbial passing of the torch from me to you."

"Okay."

"At least until you're fully ready."

"Okay."

"You'll know when this time arrives."

I nodded.

"For the time being, we will keep these conversations to this very spot, okay?"

"Okay."

One wrapped his arm back around my shoulder. He pulled me so my head rested on his arm. We sat like that for a while and my nose felt numb from the cold and One told me I was going to change the world and I didn't look up to see the whites of his eyes because I couldn't take it if they were lying.

# 28. SICK (V)

My esophagus burns at all times. Swallowing is an effort that hardly seems worth it. I try to eat rice but it's too much work. When Two uses the toilet after me, she sees my bile mixed with blood and she says it's gone too far and I say we are making progress. We shave our heads every third day. We have quit watching TV, opting for music, either Elvis or the bass-heavy trance Two likes. It feels good to see our individual ribs. Two's breasts have shrunk and her arms are little more than bone. We take turns cleaning our five-gallon buckets.

We ingest ipecac four times a day. We now swallow laxatives and stool softeners every morning. We have been doing this for a month.

It's not the same as chemo, not even close. Our regimen is more like punishment than a permanent state. But it's working because I quit thinking about having sex with Two and about getting a box spring and Two is doing well because she's quit crying about feeling sick and about Derek and she's even started asking to up her doses of everything.

Sickness bears Honesty. Honesty bears change.

We seek with as much Honesty as we can muster.

Yet we're blocked with fear and want and memories of how we wish our childhoods had been. It's time for Reprieve.

---

It feels wrong having Two buy the DMT, but she knows people and I don't. I insist on paying for it. She arrives at my apartment around ten on a Friday night. It's our fifth week of Seeking. Two's excited. She tries to hide this fact because she thinks it demonstrates selfishness. I tell her it's all good. I tell her Reprieve is both a celebration and a tool for digging deeper into Self. She tells me she's never smoked Demisters and I tell her it's easy. I turn off all the lights except for the lamp she's given me. I hold the tin foil. I tell her not to suck too hard. She laughs. She's nervous. She takes three hits. I guide her backward, her bald head a fragile egg being placed underneath a mother's warmth. It's my turn and I take four hits and the taste is my adolescence and I want One to hold me and I close my eyes and enter the void.

I'm all over the place.

I feel Jerome entering me and I feel him grab the back of my head and it's so close to One's touch and then things are dark as my face meets cinderblock. I'm mute, living in a psych ward. I'm a fifteen-year-old boy silently urging my father to climax so I'll be left alone. I'm John Doe and Mason Hues and Thirty-Seven and One. I'm a teacher. I'm a leader. I'm a boy who knows more about the world than anyone else, even One.

I think I hear crying, but I'm not sure.

The crying gets louder and I see the body that houses Two's consciousness sobbing and I know she's broken down walls that aren't supposed to be broken. I reach out and take her hand. This calms her because all we want is connection.

She tells me everything is beautiful and everything is horrible. I know exactly what she means. She tells me so much of her life has been about sex. I tell her people's loss of connection to God results in this particular perversion. She asks if I think she's pretty. I tell her she's the most beautiful woman I've ever seen. Her pinky is a grazing deer on the grasslands of my ribs.

Two says, "Was it better before?"

My eyes are only partially closed. I see Two's hipbones poking out from her jeans. They make me think of smashed dinner plates. I ask her what she's talking about.

"In Marble, with the others."

"Different."

"Different *better*?"

"Just different."

"What went wrong?"

"We thought fear could change the world."

"Fear dissipates," Two says.

"Exactly."

"Then what changes the world?"

"God," I said.

"Do you believe in God?"

"No."

"How can there be no accidents if there's no God making sure everything goes according to plan?"

My body is a supernova swallowing itself, everything exploding through contraction. It's modus ponens. Something has to play the role of God, and that something is us. I sit up at the same time as Two, both of us floating and sinking and dying and becoming immortal.

"Fuck me," Two says. "That's it. The One Truth: we're God."

# 29. GOD[8]

8 In *Dr. Sick*, O'Connor uses the words *God* and *Savior* fifty-six times. That's roughly once every ten pages. Most often, O'Connor writes about how everything Dr. Shepard did was to cement his role as Savior to first The Survivors, and secondly the world.

The only times I can remember One uttering the word *God* was in relation to love. We spoke about it one night on the boulder, as we'd taken to doing every evening since he'd started privately deferring to my judgment. For some reason, I asked what his daughter's name had been.

"Zoe."

"That's pretty."

"She was beautiful."

"Do you still miss her?"

"Every day," One said.

I nodded. He asked if I missed my family. I shook my head and then I nodded.

One said, "People are adaptable. We're programmed for it. It's how we survive."

"To lie to ourselves?" I said.

"To believe in God."

I laughed and One didn't and then I was quiet. "That's really what it's all about, you know? How else does anybody get through anything?"

"Sex and narcotics and TV," I said.

One smiled at me, but it was a pitying smile. I felt young.

"It's a shit deal, if you think about it. Life, I mean. We all die. We all hurt. We all lose. The only way any of us can get through is by turning to God. Have him take it all away." One snapped his fingers. "A hundred virgins, cloud-filled beds, reunited with everyone who has so much as smiled at you…if there's no reward, why the hell would anyone keep on?"

"But it's believing in a lie."

"It's surviving."

I threw a pebble against a tree. It made a soft *thud* and then fell into the snow. I said, "In a way, God's kind of the opposite of Truth."

"Not *God*, but people's reliance upon God, that's the opposite of Truth."

"Simple," I said, smiling. "Then all we have to do to enact change is to kill God."

One said, "You can't kill something that lives in every human."

"Then we're fucked," I said.

"You're thinking about it wrong. It's not about killing or destroying or any such violent behavior—it's about *giving*."

I didn't say anything.

"We give them the gifts they expect from a nonexistent entity."

This conversation wasn't in *Dr. Sick* because I didn't tell it to the Feds. But even if Henry O'Connor had known about this exchange, I wonder if he would have included it. To me, One's words seemed to go against the monster O'Connor painted in his book. For starters, it shows a complexity I didn't know One had in regards to his notion of God. He believed and he didn't. He wanted there to be meaning and he was scared there wasn't. He needed to think of his daughter waiting for him inside of pearly gates, but he was unable to. Secondly, O'Connor's main case was how Dr. James Shepard was a textbook cult leader, skilled in the dark arts of brainwashing in order to impart a God-like aura around his bald head. But that's not true. Yes, we loved him. Yes, we looked to him for answers. But he never once spoke about being *chosen* or *selected* or that he was even any better than the people we hid from. He lived by a simple doctrine aimed to conduct an Honest life surrounded by a loving family of his own choosing. The other stuff—The Notes, the DEA agents, The Day of Gifts—came after something genuine was lost.

Sometimes I wonder if it was my showing up.

Dr. Turner had a different take on God. She talked about how God was synonymous with guilt for much of the world, at least in our country. She spoke about morality, which she argued existed in each human. It could either be nurtured or left in a smoldering car in a sea of asphalt. She talked about the notion of God arising when people didn't know how to make their actions and thoughts match their ingrained morality.

I don't know, it's probably the same thing.

But my point, at least initially, is that One did not view himself as God. He believed himself to be great and to be loving and to be willing to die for what he believed was a change the world needed, but he did not believe himself capable of miracles.

This makes O'Connor's assertion not only erroneous, but interesting. I imagine he was not able to conjure any other explanation for why we showed up at One's doorstep and asked to be made sick enough to die. O'Connor couldn't fathom a world where you're given teeth of those who'd died in your house to file into dust. The sex, the Reprieves, The Day of Gifts—how else could any of this make sense unless we believed One to be God? How could a seemingly normal person destroy century's worth of societal and moral norms in the blink of a few months?

Dr. Turner would always tell me things weren't my fault, that I was a victim of abuse and cruelty and mental instability and circumstance.

Toward the end of my stay at CMHIP, I came to believe these things.

Because I'd been John Doe and then Mason Hues and then Thirty-Seven.

Because I'd wanted nothing but connection and my father couldn't brave the ten feet from the doorway to my bed.

Because I'd done unspeakable things that no longer made sense.

Because I was once again filled with want.

Five once told me there was nothing lonelier than acceptance of failure.

One once told me I was a once-in-a-millennium seeker of Truth.

Maybe the reason O'Connor insisted that Dr. James Shepard was playing the role of God was merely an act of transference. O'Connor must've imagined himself in our positions with ruined lives and distorted views of humanity, must've seen himself taking Reprieve and taking Cytoxan, being asked to break into somebody's home to leave a death threat. He couldn't imagine himself doing these things because nobody can imagine doing these things. But he kept trying, knowing he had to get deeper to the emotional core of those he wrote about, and he realized it was about trust; O'Connor couldn't think of anything he could or would trust that much besides God. So he engaged in his own faulty modus ponens and deduced we must've all seen One as a Savior.

But unlike us, O'Connor had never faced certain death and begged for it to be as long as possible, only to be guided through every stage of grief by a loving family of our own choosing, who'd gone, or were going, through the exact same thing. He'd never turned his life over to the destruction of Self. He'd never been granted the fruits of complete Honesty, The Gifts of Understanding, the tingles of ceasing to exist, the connection to unnamable Truth.

We had. We'd been given insights normally reserved for the fluttering of eyelids and retardation of hearts. We knew God was a crutch to allow people to cheat and steal and murder and fortify themselves inside of semi-customized homes in subdivisions and to withhold love and to scapegoat gluten and Muslims and homosexuals and masturbate over their sleeping children with a smile because all they had to do was feel guilt and repent.

Or maybe that's all bullshit.

Maybe I intuited that we had destroyed ourselves and became Gods.

Maybe that's why I'd felt comfortable with raping and pillaging my consciousness.

Maybe I'd struggled with this notion, keeping the One Truth hidden because I feared its power, instead allowing blame and reduced sentences and victim-based psychotherapy to fill its void.

And maybe everything happens for a reason—Two coming into my life, her yearning leading to questions, her questions leading to Truth.

# 30. PARDON

Two and I walk around town at night because sleep doesn't feel important and because we like the cold air and because we're invisible. We hold hands and sometimes arms. We're in love with our lives and how our bodies feel and maybe one another. We speak to homeless people because they have a special talent for noticing Seekers. Some of them are rude and tell Two they want to fuck her throat. But most are nice, kind, broken. Sometimes we sit with them for hours. We listen to their stories because nobody else will. They initially speak about all the ways people have screwed them. Once blame is established, they talk about plans for getting off the streets. These are heartbreaking because not even the homeless believe these stories. Sometimes, if the person has a natural inclination for Honesty, he'll tell us about what it was like before. He'll tell us about things he'd had that are now gone—job, car, big-screen TV, a family—always in that order. He'll regress here, once again casting blame, but it's a short rebuttal to Truth. He'll circle back to his soft voice. He'll say something about fucking everything up with drugs or war or drink. Sometimes he cries. These aren't selfish tears, but more about time, the loss of it, a eulogy. "Ten years," he'll say. "I've been on these streets for ten years."

One night we speak with a black guy in his mid-thirties. He looks rough, the kind that comes with rapid aging from inhaled coke. He's angry. He's angry at us because he thinks we're Nazis or maybe because we're white. It's hard to tell. White spittle crusts at the corners of his lips. He is in the blame section of his monologue. He jabs at my chest and then Two's and he tells us we're cocksuckers for not giving him money.

The skin connecting his ear is wrinkled it's pulled so tight. I'm about to tell Two we should go when she jabs the man in the chest. He is startled and instinctively reaches up to rub his sternum.

Two says, "Whatever you did—raped your little sister, shot some kid, or just pissed away everything your mom worked so hard to give you—it doesn't matter. You hear me? It. Doesn't. Fucking. Matter. Not anymore."

"Bitch, don't poke me," he says. He takes a few steps toward Two. She cocks her head and he stops and I know she is connected to a power greater than any combustion of atoms.

"It's over with," Two says. "Behind you. You no longer have to kill yourself over it. You no longer have to make it disappear. Because it's gone." She places her two fingers on the man's lower forehead, right above his wide nose. "You're forgiven for everything you've ever done or thought or wanted. You're free."

The man closes his eyes. Two presses. The man wets his lips, moving around the white globs of detritus. When his eyes open, they are clear, or clearer. They are Honest, moist. He blinks. A tear falls. His lips tremble. He tries to find words. Two shakes her head like speaking isn't necessary. She takes my hand and we walk away.

I tell her that was amazing. She tells me it had come to her, a Gift of Understanding, knowing this man was in the process of killing himself for the sins he'd committed. Two says, "And like you said, what's the biggest reason a person turns to God?"

"For the assurance everything is still okay," I say.

"Which is another way of saying *forgiveness*."

We keep walking. Two feels good about her actions. I like that she has taken ownership of this gift because it only came due to her dedication to sickness.

Now we go out every night with a purpose: to pardon the unlovable. Some of them are ready to be forgiven and some of them spit in our faces. But overall, we are making a difference. We are enacting change. We are becoming better versions of ourselves. We give gifts that only God can give. The homeless start to recognize us. The first guy whom Two had pardoned always crosses the street when he sees us, but he waves, smiles. Word spreads. An old guy with ripped pants and one eye gets off his cardboard box after we've passed by. He struggles to jog after us. He mumbles, but I understand him: "Jesus and Mary, make me better."

I press my fingers to his head.

Two holds his filthy hands.

We tell him it's all over with, his guilt, his past, every atrocity he's ever committed.

We make our way to the river. We see fire. We hear drums. We walk over and there's maybe a hundred kids spinning poi and playing drums. The air smells like skunk and dirty sheets. I watch a girl spin two flaming balls on chains around her body. She's beautiful and she has her eyes closed and isn't trying to show off. Some kids have skulls painted on their faces and they wear the baggy clothes of previous generations. One kid smashes a bottle against a playground, and then they all do, these Juggalos, these boys who hate because it's easier than being rejected. Two and I walk over. We watch them break everything they can. There's so much testosterone and so much hurt. One of the kids turns. His painted face is ghostly white and it makes me think of

Thirty-Eight. He's about to say something but stops. He smiles. His teeth are ruined from soda and neglect and crystal.

"You're them," he says.

"We're who?" I say.

"Jack and Jill."

His boys laugh and he smiles but no sound escapes.

"Those two God freaks. Yeah. You're them. You have to be."

He steps closer. He's the kind of skinny that knows how to fight. Two doesn't hold my hand even though I want her to.

"You come here to preach at me? *Save* me?"

There's laughter. A group of seven boys circles us.

"Well, here's some news for you: I don't want your bullshit religion."

I'm granted a Gift of Understanding and it's this kid growing up in Kansas, this kid one of five children and a mother who smokes in the house and a father who beats with God's Righteousness and there's Bible school and inappropriate touches and huffing paint, this kid an outsider of a dying town, this kid hearing angry music with a cult following and then everything making sense, makeup and the doctrine of nothing mattering, family.

He is me from a different tax bracket.

I feel sad. He's in my face yelling about what a piece of shit I am. I feel empathy.

"Nobody asked for your *forgiveness*," he yells.

"You didn't have to ask," I say.

"What about if I grabbed your he/she and fucked her ass? Would you still forgive me?"

I don't say anything.

Two says, "Yes, yes we would."

He laughs and it's a horrible laugh, one practiced before it became ingrained. He says, "And what about you, faggot? You still be all high and mighty if I fucked your ass?"

I take Two's hand and start walking away. I know it's not smart to turn your back on drugs and shame, but standing there isn't smart either. He calls out to us: "We'll see how godly you are." I can't decide if this is a threat or a promise.

We walk back to the river.

I'm angry. My body is a single flexed muscle. Two tells me it's not a big deal. I nod. I close my eyes and breathe out selfish fear. I bump into somebody. It's the girl I'd watched spin fire. She looks annoyed and then she looks sweet when I apologize. Two tells her she was amazing.

"Thanks, sister." The girl raises her arms to hug Two. Her armpits are hairy and she presses her face to Two's. She turns and does the same thing to me.

"Sarah," she says.

"Two."

"Two?"

"Yeah."

"Rad. You?"

"One."

"One and Two? Are you guys for real?"

Two tells her we're for real.

Sarah looks at both of us and then nods and says that's cool. Her jaw moves back and forth, but it's not out of deceit or anger— it's something chemical. She reaches out and takes our hands and she says, "One and Two," and she rubs her thumb over the back of my knuckle and I realize she's rolled.

"You guys are beautiful," she says.

"You are," Two says.

"Are you sick?"

"Not in the way you think," I say.

"But you're getting better?" Sarah says.

"Trying," Two says.

Sarah's jaw grinds back and forth. She shivers. I ask if she has a jacket and she tells us somewhere. Two starts to take off hers when Sarah stops her. She holds onto Two's arm. She says, "You were going to give me your jacket?"

Two nods.

"You're one of the few good ones, Two. Both of you."

We smile and feel warm because praise is praise.

There's some shouting from the street. Flashlights dissect the blackness. Somebody yells *five-oh*. People disperse, some walking, some running.

Sarah's eyes become wide and she flinches into herself and I know she's scared of being arrested because she's high or because she has secrets.

"This way," I say. I take Two's hand. She holds Sarah's. We are illusionists because we become invisible to the cops and even to the Juggalos throwing bottles at the oncoming policemen.

Sarah says she likes our apartment. She says it's rad how simple we live. We offer her rice and she politely declines and then I offer her Mr. Pibb and she says, "Okay, but just a little."

We sit, Two and Sarah on the mattress, me Indian-style across from them. Sarah offers to smoke us out. We don't want to seem rude so we partake. I'm not used to weed and my head becomes a contrail to a plane flying into the World Trade. Sarah talks about spinning fire. She tells us she was raised going to cheer camp and we laugh and she tells us she's serious. She tells us she left home because it was all bullshit. We don't push for details. She tells us she's been in Denver for a month. She likes it. But hates the motherfuckers on the streets. Two asks about the Juggalos. Sarah shudders. Sarah tells us she has a few more weeks before she'll head down south to Arizona for the rock and gem circuit. She says it will probably be better, living on the streets in the warm weather.

We're high and nodding and Elvis's voice sounds like a muffled plea for help from my computer speakers.

Sarah looks at me, studies me. She says, "What do you guys know that I don't?"

This is a question a Seeker would ask. I tell her we don't know much of anything, but try to live simply, Honestly.

"You guys are lucky," Sarah says. "Finding each other. Your love is out of this world strong."

Two tells her it's not like that, at least physically.

"You two aren't..."

"No," Two says.

"Why?"

"Because that sort of intimacy has a way of clouding the search for Truth," Two says. Sarah nods. I feel hurt by Two's comments even though I'm the one who's taught her this.

"Back to my question," Sarah says. "What do you two know that nobody else does?"

"I'll show you," Two says. She sits up. She takes Sarah's hand. She says, "I want you to tell me a few things. That's it. Tell me a few things about yourself, or the experiences that have shaped who you think you are."

Sarah laughs because she's suddenly nervous. But she nods. Two tells Sarah to speak directly into her ear. Sarah nods again. Two tells her to be as open and honest as she possibly can. She tells her there are no wrong answers, nothing to feel embarrassed or ashamed by. Two leans forward. Sarah leans closer to Two's head. Two asks her to describe her first love. Sarah smiles, but starts talking. She tells Two about a boy named Michael who she stated dating as a freshman and how it was different from all her friends because it was actually real. She talks about how they'd lie by the lake and not talk or even fool around, just listen to one another breathe. They dated for two years and it was magical and it was real. And then it ended, Sarah drunk at a party, Sarah drunk and stupid, Sarah sleeping with a lacrosse player who she'd never spoken to before. Two asks about her favorite memory. Sarah is closer to Two's ear, her nose touching cartilage. Sarah tells her about Christmas when she was young, probably seven or eight. She tells about her father returning from the first Gulf War and how she ran to meet him in the airport and how he held her that night, wouldn't stop loving her, wouldn't stop kissing her cheeks. Sarah's crying. Two asks about her biggest regret. Now the tears are real and angry and earnest. Sarah struggles to form words and then she's telling us about a fight she'd had with her father, how strict he was, how he tried to be a father even though he was always gone. She sobs. She says they fought before he went to Afghanistan. She can't speak. She wretches into Two's ear. Time loses the battle of rigidity because Sarah is a teenager and she's yelling at a man she'll never see again, yelling because she's scared and hormonal and wanting attention. Sarah tells Two she told her father she hoped he died.

Two holds Sarah's head.

She presses her forehead to Sarah's. She pets her hair. She keeps saying *shh*. She tells her we are not our pasts. She tells her we can change. She tells her everything—absolutely everything—happens for a reason. She tells her that those who seek Truth eventually find it. She tells her that we are living a simple life dedicated to Honesty among a loving family of our own choosing. She whispers that Sarah's father forgives her.

———

I wake up on the floor. The sun isn't out but it's close. I look at the bed. Two lies there bald and beautiful. Sarah's gone. I look around the apartment. Her pack isn't there. Neither is my computer. There's a note. It says, "*I'm sorry. You two don't deserve me.*"

I understand some people aren't ready for forgiveness. I understand nothing happens by accident, that ideas grow, especially for those searching. I hope she gets a good price for my computer. I hope she finds Truth.

I climb into bed and hold Two and she murmurs something that sounds like *love yo*u. I match the cadence of my breathing to hers. We are one with our inhales. We are nothing with our exhales.

# 31. EDICT

It was New Year's Eve and people were joyous and flirtatious and we took Reprieve around a campfire with snow falling on our bald heads. I saw bodies burning before I realized they were family members sitting across from me. I felt like water contained in a stainless-steel thermos. I thought about power and about Truth and wondered if they weren't one and the same. People were too excited and happy with themselves. Thirty and Nineteen fornicated. I wondered if maybe I was simply jealous. The vestige of bodies burning wouldn't leave my mind's eye. Things kept building and smoldering and orange was red and red was everywhere and everything tasted like bile. Sickness bears Honesty, Honesty bears change. Therefore, sickness bears change. We weren't sick. We were, but not enough, not the kind that made you pray for death or ask for help. We were drunk on our national attention. We were invisible and we wanted to be rock stars. We were nothing but preachers using fear to fulfill selfish wants.

Five came over. She wrapped her arm around me. She smiled. Her teeth had become filed from acidic coating. She was still beautiful. She asked if I was okay and I told her I was good but she didn't believe me. One came over and he put one arm around me, one around Five. We pressed foreheads. But it wasn't the same. Nothing was being transmitted by the whites of our eyes because our intentions weren't pure.

"What's wrong?" One asked.

"This isn't right," I said.

"Nothing happens by accident," One said.

"Then my understanding that we've veered off path isn't an accident."

One and Five exchanged a look.

"Reprieve is supposed to be a joyous time," Five said.

"Reprieve is supposed to be a tool to break down internal walls of Self," I said.

"Can't this wait?" One said.

"Sure," I said. "Whatever you think is best."

I went downstairs and lay on the carpet and listened to an Elvis concert from when he was fat and dying. I had my eyes closed. I was alone. I was being a baby. I was the only member of my family still seeking. I heard footsteps. I kept my eyes closed. It was One, I could tell by his breathing—always a catch on his inhale before he broached a subject he didn't want to—and I felt him staring at me, trying to access the right words.

I didn't wait for him to speak. I said, "We have lost our sickness. We have lost humility."

"I don't think that's entirely—"

"No, of course you don't."

One started to say something, but stopped.

"We need to become sick," I said.

"Okay."

"Sicker than your daughter was at the very end."

# 32. NYE

It's New Year's and we're headed to a rave in an abandoned warehouse in the old meatpacking district of Denver. We know there will be people there in need of pardon and we know there will be supplies for Reprieve. Two tells me she has a present. She digs through her backpack and tosses me something soft and black. I unfold a set of black scrubs. I smile and so does she. We change in front of one another. Two's pelvis is a dinosaur bone unearthed on a dried creek bed. She sees me watching her change and her face doesn't flinch and neither does mine.

The rave's in an old warehouse, a single massive room. Everything's concrete—floors, walls, poles reaching two stories upward—and there are probably two thousand people. Everything is muggy. A stage occupies the far end of the room. A DJ spins. Naked girls with glow-in-the-dark paint dance next to him. Lights shoot down from rafters. A disco ball the size of a car looms above oblivious heads. Kids suck pacifiers. A boy wears nothing but a set of angel wings and a girl walks around naked except for a Hello Kitty backpack. She holds a leash connected to a dildo on toy wheels.

Two says she's going to get our supplies for Reprieve. I don't want to be alone. She becomes anonymous and then she's gone. I bob my

head to the music. I watch a sea of people move to their interpreta-
tions of a communal heartbeat. Some people dance to be seen. Some
people dance with their eyes closed but still to be seen. Some people
dance to escape and they aren't themselves for song-long intervals
and these are my people because our unsaid prayer is *make it stop;
please don't let it end.* I think about these kids having done the best
they could at finding a loving family of their own choosing. Maybe
the synergy of dancing and intoxication is enough to lift them from
walls they've constructed around themselves. They forget about victimhood. They don't stress about people who've died or things they
can't afford or men they let enter them. They are momentarily free
of fear. They are free of Self. Their Truth isn't Honesty, but it's of their
own choosing, and that counts for something.

I know we possess something that can't be gained through
chemicals.

We will give our people the gift of freedom.

Two emerges from the crowd. She walks next to me. She puts
her mouth to my ear. "So, I might have made a mistake."

I look at her from the corner of my eyes.

"I mean, I got the DMT, but I also got…"

"What?"

"A little something else."

She smiles. I don't.

"It was stupid. I can throw it away."

"What part of you bought it?" I say.

"Huh?"

"Self or Honesty?"

"I don't know."

"Yes, you do."

"Honesty," she says. The skin connecting her ear pulls tight.
I nod. I tell her it's all good. Two smiles. She'd lied straight to my

face. This isn't a good way to start Reprieve. She holds up a vial of chalky powder. I ask what it is and she tells me it's a great mix. I ask her again. She tells me ketamine and crystal.

There are no accidents.

I snort two nostrils full off the back of her hand.

We smoke DMT from a glass pipe that once contained a miniature paper rose.

Everything is a slow erection.

We press our heads together.

Somebody slaps me on the back. I turn to see a spun kid smiling. He says, "So fucking rad. Your costumes. The Survivors. So cool."

Two takes my hands. She leads me into the middle of the dancing bodies or maybe body. A strobe hits. Everything is red and heavy and I'm sitting by a roaring fire three years before, ashamed to be associated with a group living so far from Honesty. Five lies to me. One lies to me. Two lies to me. Dr. Turner lies to me. My father lies to me. My mother lies to me. I lie to myself. Two holds me and we dance and my body isn't my own so I don't care. One tells me I possess a gift. One tells me I am more connected to Truth than anyone in the family. He tells me I would silently lead until I was ready. And that's what I do. I lead us to double our regular doses of Cytoxan. I lead us to sickness so absolute we lose family members whose bodies give out before their spirits, or maybe it's the other way around. Sickness bears two things: Honesty and death. I lead us head first into both. We die. We're buried fifty yards from a cliff in the mountains of Marble. Two presses her lips to my ear and I wait for her words but all I feel is her tongue. The strobe is orange or maybe blue. It emits heat and it emits longing. The only Truth for these broken kids dancing around us is the pain of their first loves and the grainy clip of their favorite memories and the weight of the actions they've committed. But that can change. We can change it. Because there are no accidents. Because I led us to the Truth of Fear in Marble. But that isn't a Truth, but rather a result of the One Truth. People fear the Sublime. People fear God. Two's hands are under my shirt and I sweat and she rubs and we are exactly the same as every person and animal and plant and God who has ever existed. People had to die. The DEA agents. Family members. The civilians during The Day of Gifts. They had to die in order to get me locked up and paroled and needing a job and meeting Talley. One said I was going to change the world—it simply was going to happen with a family of my own choosing.

We're spun kids offering pardon to other spun kids and everything is moist. We're pressing our foreheads to everyone. We're looking for Honesty and we're seeing chemicals and hurt and people trying so hard to have fun when the overriding emotion is escape. My teeth chatter. Two never lets go of my hand. I love everyone. A Mexican girl cries in Two's arms. A guy has a seizure and I cradle his head and his eyes are nothing but the whites and nothing but Truth. The massive disco ball lowers. We're chanting. We're praying the New Year will be better and our parents will love us how we need and that we'll stop shooting drugs and that we'll get a scholarship and that our boyfriends will stop meeting housewives on Craigslist and that we'll be famous for doing nothing and that there's a God and that we don't get sick and that we get sick enough to change. We scream into the night—*six, five, four*—and we scream into our pasts and this is the year we're going to find love and this is the year we're going to lose weight and this is the year we're going to get over the death of our mothers and this is the year we're going to jog and quit being whores and make amends to our ninth-grade girlfriends and we're one mind and one voice—*three, two, one*—and I feel everything at once, every thought and history and want, every fear and insecurity and sexual desire masquerading as a joke, everything, all of it, because I possess the One Truth and because I am a once-in-a-millennium Seeker and because I am God in human form or at least a human who knows God is nothing but consciousness and logic and subtle body language tells.

It's the New Year.

We're surrounded by people who want what we have.

We're building a loving family of our own choosing.

The rave's still going, but Two and I are done. We walk into the winter air. We're excited. We're high. We are experiencing the pleasures of living in Honesty. Two's given out her number to a bunch of kids who understood we were different. It's all a matter of time.

We walk on a sidewalk with chunks missing. A light snow falls. We shiver but don't care. It's dark and pretty and maybe perfect.

I hear a bottle breaking behind us.

I turn around to see a few kids. They are nothing but shapes of shadows. Two holds my hand tighter. We keep walking. We hear them calling out to us. Another bottle breaks, this time closer, ten feet away. I think about turning around and telling them to fuck off and then I think about running.

A third bottle explodes at our feet.

"Told you God faggots I'd find you."

I know it's the Juggalo kid from the night we met Sarah.

"I'm talking to you two."

We walk faster.

There's laughter and the echoes of shoes hitting pavement. A final bottle breaks at our feet. My pants are covered in cheap liquor. We stop because that's our best option. Two squeezes my hand. It's two kids, their faces painted white and black, skeletons or demons or people trying to enact change through fear.

"Kind of rude," the kid says. "Walking away when somebody's talking to you."

We don't respond.

He's three feet away. I smell alcohol. I am granted a Gift of Understanding about this substance's effects on his life—abuse and neglect and stealing his mother's wallet from her purse as she's passed out on the couch at noon—and I know it grants him the freedom to be his father and to partake in violence and to pretend death isn't imminent.

"I'm just trying to talk to you," he says. His smile is hideous poking through his painted mask. His friend laughs. He says, "I need forgiveness."

"You're forgiven," Two says.

They both laugh.

"You feel that?" he says. His friend keeps laughing. The kids says, "I'm a new man. A new fucking man. Thank you, thank you. I'm healed. I'm saved."

"See the light," his friend says.

They both laugh. We back up. My heart is the bass from the warehouse. I feel afraid.

"Just one question," the kid says. He puts out his hand for us to stop. He makes his skeleton face serious. "Can you give me forgiveness for something I haven't done yet?"

I register his movement a moment late, and then it's a flashing of green and then everything is white armfuls of laundered sheets and then there's pain and sound and maybe it's me, a groan that sounds like an echo of a scream, glass shattering over my face, things darkening.

I fall to the pavement.

Two's screams change from shock to fear.

I can't move and maybe I'm dying and I taste metal. I fight to keep my eyes open. I'm lying in bed begging for death. One is asking me if I really want to die. He's asking if I want to live a life dedicated to Honesty. He's asking if I want to be supported by a loving family of my own choosing. I'm a child face down in a kiddy pool. I'm nothing but fear. I can't see because I'm buried fifty feet from a cliff with no teeth. But I know what they are doing to Two because he'd told us and these kids understand the fraction of Truth that nothing matters besides the moment.

Two screams. She starts saying *no*. It's the mantra we'd all given as the ball dropped; it's the only mantra anyone ever really gives.

My world is jagged shapes and fluid lines.

I feel sharpness digging into my palm.

Light creeps in through the corners of my eyes.

I'm able to move.

I'm holding a sliver of the bottle smashed over my head. I'm kneeling and I'm sick and I'm trying to find a bucket and I'm cold and my teeth ache and I'm hiking through Marble in search of something real. Two is face down against the sidewalk, her scrubs pulled down. One kid sits on her back. The kid who'd hit me kneels behind her. He masturbates in order to get hard. He spreads open her butt cheeks with his free hand. His face changes from a skeleton to a white trash kid who wants to spread his pain. I'm thinking about everything happening for a reason and dead federal agents and about the only woman I'd ever loved being raped and then about my father's face in the same communion with God as he masturbated over my sleeping body.

I slam the glass into the neck of the guy sitting on her.

I look down.

The other kid has his penis pressed into Two. He looks up at me. The whites of his eyes match his face paint. He's granted a Gift of Understanding as I lunge toward him. He shows no remorse; I offer no forgiveness. I'm jamming the glass into his throat again and again and again and again and I'm hearing Elvis sing "Blue Moon" and then everything is calm and he bleeds and Two bleeds and I bleed.

I've left notes promising the death of small children.

I've pulled teeth from eight people.

I've sawed off the feet of two DEA agents.

But these are the first lives I've taken.

Sickness bears Honesty; Honesty bears change; change results in death. I hadn't been ready to accept this Truth in Marble. I'd left the day before The Day of Gifts.

There are no accidents.

We are Gods dressed in decaying flesh.

Two pulls up her pants. She's done crying. She spits on the faces of the dead. She takes my hand and helps me to my feet. I remember Five doing the same with One. Everything is really the search for love. I have the wherewithal to take the sliver of glass I'd used to enact change. Two presses her forehead to mine. She says, "I love you so fucking much."

I don't tell people I love them because it normally isn't True or maybe because they will eventually let me down or maybe because I'd never thought love was real. But this is different. Because I know it's the most Honest thing I've ever uttered: "I love you too."

# 33. BURIED

We got sick and some people complained and some people tried to leave and some people died. A respiratory infection swept through our home. Almost all of us had doubled both the regularity and amount of Cytoxan. One spoke for me. He said our senses of Self had become inflated after our enacted change from The Notes. He said he could see want and fear in the whites of all of our eyes.

The first things to fall off were chores.

We simply were too sick. All of us. At the same time. There weren't the checks and balances of staggered stages of chemo. We all extended our arms on the same days. We all prayed for death on the same nights. We expelled poison from every orifice. A lot of us cried. We didn't wash our sheets. We didn't switch beds every night. We lay there and were lucky to not soil ourselves. Dishes piled up. Toilets were splattered with dark matter. We blamed one another until we quit caring.

After two weeks of my new edict, I heard shouting. It was Twenty-Nine. He yelled because he didn't want to be injected and because he was too sick and because he was scared he was going to die. One tried to calm him. He told Twenty-Nine it was selfish fear speaking, not Twenty-Nine. He said that sickness bore Honesty. He said we all loved him.

"Fuck you. Fuck this place."

We were scared and we were sorry and we didn't give a shit.

One said that he'd give Twenty-Nine a ride to town. Twenty-Nine told him not to bother, but One insisted.

One came back three hours later. He looked at me. I wanted him to tell me how it went and I wanted him to tell me I hadn't ruined our family. One's boots were wet and muddy. And then I was granted a Gift of Understanding—Twenty-Nine's final destination being buried by the cliffs instead of the Greyhound station—and I wasn't scared or ashamed and the only word that crossed my mind was *good*.[9]

---

9 According to Henry O'Connor, there were nine bodies, or nine different *portions* of bodies, buried 1.25 miles away from Dr. James Shepard's Colorado estate. Six men, three women. Five of the bodies could be identified through forensic means. Of those five people, all of them had been reported missing sometime over the three-year period from 2011–2014. The causes of death were indeterminable, except for two of the bodies, which showed blunt force trauma to the cranium.

I know at least one of the blunt force trauma bodies was Thirty-Eight's.

The other was probably Twenty-Nine's.

One had told me that his wife had left him after their daughter, Zoe, passed. I didn't question this because I'd heard of couples disintegrating after dead children. But sitting in CMHIP, poring over the pages of *Dr. Sick*, I read the chapter "Graveyard" for the first time. O'Connor writes: "Only one of nine bodies buried in Shepard's backyard contained its teeth. That body belonged to Patti Stein Shepard, Dr. James Shepard's wife of two decades, who had been missing for six years, ever since a trip to France from which she never returned."

I talked about this with Dr. Turner.

I was shaken up and told her it was bullshit, O'Connor's book, the detail about One's wife.

"Facts are facts, Mason."

"Facts aren't facts."

"I'm afraid I'm not following."

I wasn't either. My head hurt or maybe felt congested. There had to be a mistake; there had to be a reason.

"It doesn't mean One killed her."

"Please, let us refer to *One* as Dr. Shepard."

"This doesn't prove that *One* killed her. She could've…"

"Yes?"

I was at a loss for words; I was at a loss for self-preserving rationale. It was at this moment when things started to crack. Or maybe they were long-since fractured, and this was when other voices filled those fissures with mold-producing half-truths.

Looking back, I'm not sure why I found it so hard to believe One would've killed his wife. I know he killed Thirty-Eight and Twenty-Nine. I saw him kill two DEA agents. I was instructed by him to partake in The Day of Gifts. But that's not even it. No, I now know how easily life can be taken. I know that small things happen and circumstances warrant reactions and reactions can cost lives. I know because I've done it. I was trying to change the world through giving those in need freedom from shame. I was trying to give Two a different life, one with meaning, one that lead to Truth instead of consumerism and the cannibalization of others. And I acted out of Honesty—primal, very-base-of-the-brain-stem Honesty—when I killed those Juggalos, who would've done the same to us.

There are no accidents.

Or maybe everything is an accident and life is nothing but creating narratives that force these accidents into meaning.

Dr. Turner always spoke about a *loose and broad narrative.*

I countered her arguments by saying the only reason a person listens to another person's story is to see how it relates to him, or at the most to see how he would've reacted under the same circumstances.

"You're a very bright young man, Mason."

"Thank you."

"You will be able to do anything you want with your life."

"Okay."

"Why hold yourself back with these worldviews? Why continue to be a victim? Why give Dr. Shepard that much power over you, after all that has come forth, after all the damage and heartache he has caused?"

I didn't have an answer for her. Maybe I still don't.

Dr. Turner used the momentum of "Graveyard" to systematically attack my view of One through character assassination. She made me highlight every incongruence between what Dr. Shepard had told me and what the "facts" of his life really were. She made me write down

the moments when I'd felt certain Dr. Shepard's actions didn't match up
with what he preached. One afternoon, she thought herself clever, and
asked what Dr. Shepard had said about preachers.

"Don't trust a single word that comes out of their mouths."

"And what was Dr. Shepard doing?"

"Preaching."

Dr. Turner asked me how I knew if anything Dr. Shepard had
preached was True. I knew the answer, but it wasn't coming to me because I was ruined with antipsychotics. I shrugged.

"Can you honestly sit here and tell me what you learned in that cult
makes sense?"

"No."

"Let me try it your way," Dr. Turner said. "Dr. James Shepard said
sickness bears Honesty, yet, as we all know, at the time of his apprehen-
sion, there wasn't even a trace of Cytoxan in his system. So we know he
wasn't sick. Therefore, what he said couldn't be Honest, correct?"

"I don't know."

"How can somebody profess the Truth if he isn't Honest?"

"I don't know."

"Yes, you do."

"He can't."

I went through months of soul searching or maybe trying to forget
or maybe listening to other people's views, trying them on as my own.
I didn't feel as bad about having talked to the Feds because my thirty
months were almost up and One was a liar anyway. I started to smile a
little more. I even laughed on Friday nights when we were allowed to
vote on a movie to watch in the rec room. Dr. Turner promised me that
I'd be able to serve the remainder of my sentence in CMHIP. I composed
letters to my mother about why I'd run away. I wrote letters to my father
about how his actions had devalued my life. I read these to Dr. Turner.
We didn't send them, but she promised it was therapeutic. My hair grew.
Dr. Turner asked if maybe I'd read *Dr. Sick* enough times. I told her it
helped me see Dr. Shepard for who he really was. Months passed. I was
getting better and I was getting older and I was glad to gain weight and
to not throw up and to not hear Elvis.

Two months before my eighteenth birthday, Dr. Turner and I were
talking outside. This was a rare privilege. The sun was out. Birds chirped.
I noticed these things because I'd been deprived of them for so long.
We discussed *closure*. I was telling her that I was feeling some sense of
closure with the events I'd experienced in Marble. She smiled. I wanted
her to be my mother or lover or father.

She said, "It's an amazing feeling, closure."

"For sure."

"Everyone deserves it."

I nodded.

"You're so close. Right at the precipice." She paused, as if struck by a thought. She said, "Where are the others buried?"

"What others?"

"The DEA agents Dr. Shepard killed?"

I looked into Dr. Turner's eyes. They weren't Honest. The skin connecting her ear was tight with anticipation. I was granted a Gift of Understanding—my first in over two years—and it was her selfishly wanting my recovery for herself, a career case, publication in journals and then a book, and I knew she'd made this her capstone moment, both in real life and in her future book, the moment her reformed Survivor opened up, confessed to murders and locations of federal agents, thus providing *closure* to the cult, her hard work and brilliance getting me to overcome my past atrocities. I knew nothing over the past year had been Honest. I knew I'd swallowed her bullshit because it was easier than feeling alienated from Truth. I knew I'd embraced selfish wants to crowd out selfish fears.

"I have no idea what you're talking about," I said.

"We're past that, Mason."

"Don't call me Mason."

"Why not?"

"Because that's what my father called me."

Dr. Turner nodded. She said, "Then what shall I call you?"

"Thirty-Seven."

"Why can't you tell me where the DEA agents are buried?"

"Because I don't know what you're talking about?"

"Why? You were there, weren't you?"

"Yes. But not that day."

"Why?"

"I was sick. The whole day."

"Mason—"

"Don't call me that."

"Does it strike you as odd that you were never around in times of violence?"

"There are no accidents."

"What happened the night you ran away?"

"I found a loving family dedicated to changing the world. I embraced sickness. I started living in Hon—"

"Enough!" Dr. Turner yelled.

Birds flew away. I shook. Dr. Turner closed her eyes. She knew she'd ruined everything. I thought about there being no accidents, only actions revealing hidden, detestable traits. She started to apologize, but I put up my hand. I shook my head. I got off the bench and walked inside. Three days later, I was transferred back to juvie. I looked for Dr. Turner, but she was nowhere to be found. I wasn't upset about being transferred, because it confirmed my beliefs about Dr. Turner. It confirmed the notion that a life spent dedicated to Honesty comes with gifts. It confirmed that everything I'd learned in Marble was True.

# 34. QUARTERED

One morning, I heard an old-fashioned doorbell. I was sick in bed. I hadn't showered in close to a week. My sheets had my outline in sick. I closed my eyes, willing the sound to go away. But then I heard commotion, bodies moving, voices.

I crawled out from bed. I stumbled down the hallway. My family members rushed past me. The doorbell kept ringing. The family room was vacant. I looked around for One; he was nowhere to be seen. Everything hurt. My hearing was nothing but the thrashing of nausea. I made my way to the door. I peeked outside and saw two people, a man and a woman, both dressed in suits, the man's hair slicked, the woman manly but pretty or maybe pretty because she was manly. They wore black windbreakers.

I opened the door.

They stared at me. I felt small and in need of protection

The woman's skin by her ear was pulled tight. She reached to her hip. Something wasn't right. The man's energy pushed forward, or maybe he simply rocked on the balls of his feet. He asked for Dr. James Shepard.

I looked behind me to the empty living room. I turned back to the two people. My mind wouldn't work. I wasn't granted any Gifts of Understanding because I was dying and wanted to be asleep in my childhood bed with my father watching over me. I sensed something bad was about to happen, but these were the dulled observations of the soulless: the windbreakers, the woman's hand resting on her hip, the man waving some sort of open wallet in my face. I heard "DEA" but this acronym meant nothing to me.

Then the woman had a pistol pointed at me.

Part of me welcomed the sight.

But then I saw a vision, a Gift of Understanding.

I saw One walking from the left. He was shirtless in the snow. He held a pistol. He looked beautiful against the gray sky. I understood he was protecting us, and this felt like love. He crept until the woman noticed and then she dropped to the ground and then I heard a deafening *pop* and then everything was red and there were more explosions of sound and then the man in the suit was down and One stood over both of them and I was covered in blood and I realized it hadn't been a vision, but a form of reality where One had just murdered two Drug Enforcement Agents on our doorstep. Their blood soaked into our welcome mat. I'd stood in the exact same spot and peered at Five stroking a dying man. I'd wanted everything they had. I'd wanted to be part of a family. I'd wanted a father.

One was as calm as I'd ever see him. He chambered his pistol. His hairless body was covered in blood. He looked down at me. He grabbed the back of my neck. He pressed his forehead to mine. He told me it had started. He told me it was only going to get more Honest. He told me they'd keep coming and they wouldn't stop. He told me the only True Enemies were those who didn't believe as others did. He told me there were no accidents. He told me we had been given Truth, and we were now changed, and there was no going back.

"What Truth?" I said.

"That nothing matters."

I looked down at the bleeding agents. The woman's eyes were open and they were blue and pretty and dull.

One said, "Consciousness. It's not real. It's our attempt to connect to God. God isn't real. Therefore, consciousness isn't real. None of this matters. Not a single fucking thing."

All I had wanted was to be away from my father's silent abuse.

Or maybe I'd wanted love.

Or maybe I'd wanted meaning.

Or maybe I'd wanted a loving family of my own choosing.

Or maybe I'd simply been looking for a surrogate father who would have the courage to touch me.

One said, "You led me to this Truth. You did, Thirty-Seven, with your dedication to the Honest Life."

I nodded against his bloody forehead.

He said, "None of this is real. Nothing matters. Nothing. *We* are nothing. There *is* nothing. Don't you see? Everything you've done, everything we've gone through, it all led us to this very moment. To this Truth: Nothing we do matters. And it is our duty to bring this Truth to the masses."[10]

---

10 O'Connor spends a goodly amount of page space in *Dr. Sick* on Agent Samantha Grimes and Agent Stanley Wolfe. He circles back to the investigation and raid of YYCIM Laboratories in Hoboken, New Jersey. He discusses loose ends being tied up, one of those being a loft in downtown Denver where inconsequential shipments of DMT had been sent. He talks about paper trails leading Agent Grimes and Agent Wolfe to Marble, Colorado. Here O'Connor takes certain journalistic liberties, dipping into the agents' mindsets on their trip to the mountains. He imagines their conversation. He paints a picture of nonchalance—annoyance even—at having to cross t's and dot i's. I suppose there's some truth to that, because why else would the DEA ever show up with only two agents?

Nothing has ever been proven, so O'Connor makes it clear their murder scene is conjecture. But nobody reading a nonfiction book

---

I sat on the steps for hours. I didn't say much and neither did One. Everyone else was inside, where Five tried to calm them. One quartered each agent with a hacksaw. The foot of snow at our doorstep had melted from the warm blood. One asked if I could help with the teeth. I took needle-nose pliers and pried and pried and pried. The woman's molars were stubborn. One wrapped each quarter of body in cellophane and then two black trash bags. The sun fell behind the mountains. The bags were lined up in a neat row.

One recruited six others.

We climbed inside of his Jeep and drove seven miles up the canyon. From there, we got out, our quarter of a person in backpacks made of packing tape. We walked through the snow on a trail that wasn't really a trail, but a game path with elk droppings

---

makes those distinctions. They believe what O'Connor writes. They think it was all premeditated. Like we knew they were coming. Like we *lured* them there. Like Dr. James Shepard was that much of a genius to drop a trail of bread crumbs. O'Connor writes, "The Myth of Persecution came to fruition on February third. The unseen enemies of The Survivors literally showed up at their doorstep, guns drawn. Everything Shepard had prophesized became a reality in that moment. Any doubts The Survivors may have silently harbored were dispelled. Their Savior had foreseen the future. In turn, the brainwashed had a single option: defend themselves."

The bodies still haven't been found. During my arraignment, they grilled me incessantly about the agents' deaths. I suppose it's a code, looking out for their own. I told them I had no idea; I'd been sick—really sick, sick-like-almost-dead sick—and hadn't known about any of it. They didn't believe me, but then they did because I stared at them and took their verbal threats without blinking.

After The Day of Gifts, after everything was over and the cabin was smoldering, they combed the grounds. They found two teeth, one incisor and one molar. His and hers. I'm not sure why I'd thrown them in the fire. Part of me might have thought they'd burn, but that's probably bullshit. Maybe I simply wanted the Truth to come out.

dotting the snow. We hiked for four hours. We got sick. Eleven fainted. We pushed on. There was no light that night. We kept going and then we were at a cliff and we had to use our hands to climb and everything ached.

We reached a cave. One told us it was an abandoned mine where they'd searched for slabs of marble. The cave was probably fifteen feet deep. We walked to the back. There was a rusted metal gate covering a hole. We lifted the gate. One told us the hole was at least fifty feet. He pointed to me. I dropped the pelvis of the male agent down. We listened for a thud, which came later than any of us expected. We disposed of the bodies. We arranged the gate. We sat on the cave's lip and stared at nothing and everything and we didn't cry because we weren't selfish. An owl hooted. We were a single mind. One put his arm around my shoulder. He didn't tell me he was proud, but I knew. He'd told me it was my dedication to Honesty that led him to his Gift of Understanding about consciousness being our attempt to connect to God and God not being real, so therefore consciousness wasn't real. Which meant nothing was real. Or maybe everything was real, but nothing mattered.

One spoke to the seven of us up on that ledge: "We're going to change the world."

We nodded.

I couldn't help but smile.

I said, "We're going to give them an invaluable gift."

"I like that," One said. "The Day of Gifts."

# 35. VIRGINITY

I'm telling Two that there are no accidents and we did what we had to do and we acted in self-defense and we are blameless, which doesn't even matter because blame is rooted in the Judeo-Christian bullshit of shame.

Two doesn't respond.

We're in our apartment. We're on my mattress with no box spring.

I reach out and hold her hand. She won't meet my gaze. I tell her we could go to the police this very moment, and it'd be hard, but we'd come out okay because what we said was True.

Two speaks to her lap: "I had a Gift of Understanding."

"What? When?"

"While that motherfucker..."

"It's over with."

"I saw you kill him."

"It was self-defense. Any jury would believe that. Some homeless Juggalo raping you, after trying to *kill* me with a bottle?"

"Before you did it."

"Before what? What are you talking about?"

"When he thrust himself into me, I saw you rising from the ground. I saw you slit his throat. But my eyes were closed. Then the next thing I know, they're both dead."

I reach out and try to comfort Two. She's rigid in my arms so I let go. I tell her that was what happened and the mind has a way of making fiction out of trauma and I tell her I'm sorry for everything.

"I saw the future," she says.

"It doesn't matter."

"It does."

"Why?"

"Because we really are Gods."

"We already knew that," I say.

"Maybe. I mean, I said it, but I didn't *believe it* believe it. But it's True."

"We didn't do anything wrong."

"It doesn't matter."

"Right, it's behind us. No proof. Not like we have any connection to—"

"That's not what I mean," Two says.

"Then what?"

"I mean we can do whatever the fuck we want."

I'm thinking about One saying the same thing. I'm thinking about murder provoking the same mindset. I'm thinking about our rationales for doing unspeakable actions and I'm thinking about how One was so close to arriving at the One Truth and how I needed to see his failures to be open to it with Two.

"Because we're living in Honesty," I say.

"Because we're all Gods, but we're the only motherfuckers brave enough to shoulder this responsibility."

Two finally looks up. Her eyes are pure but broken. She smiles a smile that isn't hers. She reaches out her hand and cups my face. Then the other hand. She leans forward. I ready myself for her forehead, but it's her lips. We kiss awkwardly until we forget ourselves and then our tongues are furious and calm and those of serpents.

I've never been with a woman. I feel nervous and insecure and like my penis isn't big enough. My hands are arthritic. I worry this will ruin everything. Two moans like she's drowning. She takes off my shirt and traces each of my ribs with her tongue. Her nipples are puffy in my mouth and then they harden. Our hips rub in a painful way. Her neck arches and it's vulnerable and alive and her body is warm to the touch. My fingers are colonialists along the Amazon. Her vagina is wet and I realize it's blood from the rape and I think about AIDS and this being immoral and she tells me to fill her. Her body tastes like sleep. She winces. She tells me to go slow. I do. She tells me she loves me and I believe her. She rides me and presses her forehead to mine and I tell her I love her more than anything and she looks into the whites of my eyes for Honesty and she finds it and tells me to fuck her. I think about Jerome and One and my father. I think of Dr. Turner and Five and my mother. I think about living a normal life and forgetting about all of this—sickness for the sake of Honesty, Honesty for the sake of change. Truth, fucking Truth, who cares about what is True and what is False because it doesn't matter, and not in the sense of nothing mattering because we were Gods, but because it straight up doesn't matter, as in isn't our problem, them, anyone else, the world, as in it doesn't make a single bit of difference if Truth is uncovered or closeted because I am still me, still human, still a boy with issues deeper than chemo can eradicate, still a shitting, breathing, wanting creature in desperate need of love.

And I've found it, love, the type that doesn't exist in the real world or even in movies, the kind born from the shattering of Self, and offering up those scraps to another person, the kind shrouded in temperance.

My body flexes and Two stares into my eyes and I want them to be pure and Honest and they are because she's crying and there are no accidents and we understand how everything works and we can foresee the future and we can change the world and Two says she loves me and I come into her and she collapses over my body and we breathe into one another's ears and it's our first loves and favorite memories and biggest regrets and we are free of everything that has ever happened or ever will and we are in love.

# 36. ONE'S CONFESSIONS

That night, we all gathered around the campfire. One hadn't showered. His hands were stained red, but not bloody, just a different hue of pink. The fire reached higher than normal. Some of us cried and some of us got sick and some of us were steeled over from exhaustion and complicity at having dropped our quarter of a body down an abandoned mine shaft.

One stood. He discarded his canvas jacket. He tossed his bloodied black scrub top into the flames. He walked while we sat. He looked into our eyes. Some of us met his gaze; some of us studied our cuticles.

"There are no accidents," One said.

We nodded.

One yelled it again, "There. Are. No. Fucking. Accidents."

The flames crackled. Some of us shivered. We all watched.

"I have told you this. I have demonstrated this. I have seen this Truth play out time and again. Everything—absolutely every single fucking thing—happens for a reason for those who seek Truth."

One's back was to me. The flames danced across the nubs of his spine. He walked around the far side of the fire.

"Today, they came for us. They came for us because they are afraid. Afraid of what we know. Afraid of how we live. Afraid of sickness. Of Honesty. Of change."

We nodded.

"These two were only the first. They will keep coming. They will come with SWAT teams. Helicopters. Machine guns. They will not quit. Not until we are dead. They will keep coming until we have been extinguished, solved, eradicated. They will murder us because they fear change. They fear Truth. They fear anything that will cast a shadow of doubt on their bullshit lives."

One rounded the far side of the fire. His hairless chest was splattered in blood. He was beautiful and perfect and flawed beyond reason.

"It's over," One said. "This life up here, this Utopia, this loving family of our own choosing—it's over."

Somebody said it wasn't. Somebody cried. One put his index to his lips. We were quiet. The logs crackled.

"We have lived for three years in servitude to Honesty. We will not start engaging in selfish forms of denial at this point."

He looked down at me and this made my insides warm.

"It's over. That is the very nature of Truth. It is the most combustible entity in the world. It cannot be contained. It can't be withheld. It arrives and it consumes and it is gone. We are vessels. We are the sacrificial conduits for Truth."

Our breathing quickened. Our fingers rubbed against any smooth surface. We believed.

"But this does not mean we cannot enact change."

Our heads nodded, a few of us letting out murmurs of agreement.

"We will give the Gift of Truth to the world. It will be the last thing we do. And it will be beautiful. It will be earth-shattering. It will be profane and profound and it will be sublime and it will be Honest."

We found our voices and we shouted and we felt called upon and we felt like heroes and we forgot selfish fears.

One pointed to Five sitting next to me. He said, "Five, it wasn't an accident your husband died of cancer." One pointed to Twelve. He said, "Twelve, it wasn't an accident your family was killed by a drunk driver." He stepped closer to me and stared into the whites of my eyes and his were orange from the flames and he said, "Thirty-Seven, it was no accident your birth mother handed you over to a lecherous man who only housed you to fulfill his sexual perversions."

I nodded; we all nodded.

"None of these things were accidents because they set us on a path of suffering, of sickness, of yearning. They led us to find one another. They led us here. They led us to bury our brothers and sisters. They led us to epiphanies. They led us to pray for death. They led us to Honesty. And then to Truth. They led us to fucking Truth. And we each possess it. It burns within us. Every time we've gotten sick and every time we've prayed to a God that doesn't exist, we've come closer. And now it's here. I see it in each of your eyes. We are ready. Honesty bears change. We are changed. We are no longer mortal. We are no longer meant for this earth. We have to spread this gift to those trapped in the daily bullshit of want. We have to open eyes. We have to change the fucking world."

We screamed because we knew he spoke Truth and because we felt it, this Truth, the transitory nature of everything, how consciousness was nothing but want and fear, how we were above this, how we were so close to death.

"Tonight, we take our final Reprieve. We celebrate Fate. We toast Honesty. We embrace Truth. And tomorrow, we make good on our notes."

One threw baggies of DMT at us. We were children underneath a split piñata. One took off his pants. Somebody gave me tin foil. Five's shirt was off. Others too—breasts and penises and hairless vaginas—and we yelled sounds that hadn't been heard since Jesus cried on a cross. Smoke entered our lungs. Flames consumed our bodies. Hands groped flesh. Everything was red and beautiful and Honest. Somebody's finger went inside of me. My mind was a metal saw grinding through tendons and bone. Elvis haunted my ears. We were going to die but it didn't matter because we'd all begged for finality for years. We were a single body and we were bile and ribs and sick. We would change the world. We, we, we. We kept smoking and Reprieve was never going to end and I'd thought it was about fear and maybe it was and maybe it was about family and maybe it was about companionship and maybe it was about change. I floated above us all. I floated above the mountains. I floated like a cloud laced with thorny rosebuds. I watched my family slither around trampled snow, nothing our own, nothing belonging to Self, orifices being filled because they needed to be filled. I stood off in the distance. I was naked. I touched myself to the images of those who both knew and didn't know they were being watched. I wanted to be included, but I couldn't bridge the gap. I masturbated to the thought of my father and of One and of Five holding my hand in the ocean and of people lying straight to my face and of being chosen and of being made up entirely of a combustible substance.

Later, One brought me to the boulder. It was nearly morning. We would start leaving in an hour's time. We shared a blanket. Our bare shoulders touched. He'd told me he wanted to gift me something. I waited. Finally, he spoke: "I want your Day of Gifts to be somebody specific."

"Huh?"

"Not random, like the others."

"Okay."

"Consider it a *gift with a perk*."

I looked up. One smiled, so I did too.

"I want you to give your gift to your mother."

I swallowed with no saliva.

"Yes," One said. "It's time to kill your father."

I didn't know what to say or what to think. One lowered his fore-head to mine and we pressed. We stayed like that for millennia. Then he let up and I did too and he told me to stay in the same position. I felt his mouth on my ear. He breathed in and out and it was like a vacuum and like a lullaby.

He said, "My first love was Patti. She was beautiful. Stunning. A smile like you wouldn't believe. Zoe's smile. She wouldn't even talk to me. I pursued her for three years, pretty much the entirety of col-lege. Finally, finally, she agreed to have coffee with me. We sat in the student union. I was so nervous. It was like she was doing me a favor. Hell, maybe she was. I was at a complete loss for anything to say. I ended up blurting out the first thing that crossed my mind. I said, 'What's your favorite memory?' Something changed at that point."

One pressed harder with his mouth. His tongue flicked inside of my cavern.

"My favorite memory occurred here. We'd just purchased this place as our second home. We were young, Zoe a toddler. But things were starting to happen. Our efforts were paying off. Work was going well, our marriage, our family. The first night we stayed here, we built a campfire. It was chilly, but we were cozy. Zoe and I looked everywhere for the perfect sticks to roast marshmallows. She'd never had a s'more, never roasted marshmallows. Her face... the sheer shock and awe and delight when she bit into it...it was the happiest face I've ever seen. Zoe looked at her mother and I, and didn't say anything, but conveyed that she was grateful that we were her parents and this was her life."

One's tears dripped down my bald head. Phlegm rattled in his throat.

"My biggest regret is that it all turned out this way. That this is the Truth we arrived at."

# 37. THIRTY-SEVEN

I was John Doe before I was Mason Hues before I was Thirty-Seven.

One said you could never outrun your past, but you could destroy the person you'd been through sickness and Honesty.

I left home when I was fifteen. I left home because my adopted parents loved me in an unsustainable fashion. One never talked about sustainability, which I think was a mistake. Sometimes I think everything is about sustainability. Everything is finite; everything can be exhausted. Maybe all the work we did to live in Honesty thrust us to a Truth normally reserved for the dying.

Dr. Turner told me it was normal to want things. She told me every living creature experienced wants, that it was what kept us alive. I told her it was different when all of our essential needs were met and our wants turned material and cosmetic thus outreaching our ingrained desire to survive. She asked what I wanted. I told her a loving family of my own choosing. She told me that desire was neither material nor cosmetic. She told me that was natural, my right. She told me that want was right there with food and shelter. She told me pack animals couldn't survive without it.

This story isn't about One. It's not about Dr. James Shepard. It's not about my father.

A connecting thread throughout all of *Dr. Sick: The Survivors and The Day of Gifts* is the loss and search and establishment of family. He discusses how the founding members of The Survivors were all part of the same support group for people who'd lost family members to cancer. I didn't know this until I read it. But it makes sense. They had lost children and lovers to an invisible disease. They wanted there to be a reason. They wanted to feel closer to their dead daughters. They wanted a doctrine to live by. They wanted to recreate what they'd taken for granted through complaints and neglect and affairs.

Perhaps the only reason One told me I was more connected to Truth than any of the others was to inflate my ego so I didn't tell the family about seeing Five slip out of his room. Perhaps I let this notion of superiority go straight to my head. Perhaps I experienced a sense of power for the first time in my life. And like God, I saw that it was good, and wanted more. I told One we needed to double our doses of Cytoxan. We all did. Perhaps this was unsustainable.

Dr. Turner didn't let me speak in the first person plural. Then she didn't let me talk about what we'd experienced in the mountains of Colorado. She let me speak about One, but only in relation to my own father.

Jerome had been popped for shooting a man in the chest. The man didn't die, but Jerome was sentenced to forty-one months in juvie. He was fourteen. He told me the man was his stepfather. I asked why he'd shot him. We were naked in the bottom bunk. We'd just been intimate. Jerome's skin connecting his ear tightened. He grabbed the back of my head and smashed it repeatedly against the concrete wall.

Dr. Turner spoke about a hierarchy of needs. This concept made sense to me. It wasn't Truth, but it was Honest.

Every time I hear "Blue Moon," I cry.

One always said that people just want to belong. Dr. Turner said cults use a loose and broad narrative to allow those being brainwashed to feel included. O'Connor wrote about how The Survivors underwent the same near-death experiences, eliminating any differences between themselves, thus creating a cohesive grouping, a loving family of their own choosing.

Dr. Turner disagreed with me about One's three defining aspects of a person's character. She told me we were so much more than our first love, favorite memory, and biggest regret. She told me genetics played a large role. She told me about the circumstances we were born into. She told me about how people change, constantly—the birth of children, the death of parents, the accomplishment of goals—and she told me I was too young to subscribe to the notion of my character already being set. I told her she was wrong. She looked amused. I said, "These moments are about Truth." She told me that viewed in that context, *everything* was about Truth. I said, "Your first love is about the Truth of Others, your favorite memory is about the Truth of Time, and your biggest regret is about the Truth of Yourself." She asked what that particular Truth was for me. I said, "That everything ends in a way you don't want it to."

# 38. PROPHET

We loaded into One's Jeep and the DEA's sedan. We took three trips into Glenwood Springs. We were given money for bus fare. People stared at our bald heads. They probably thought we were some chemo support group. We were past the point of caring. We hugged. Some of us hitchhiked out of town. There were tears. Some of us were scared. I waited with a few others at the Greyhound station. One told us he and Five were going to ditch the DEA car. One said they'd be back in thirty minutes, definitely before the last of our buses left.

I looked up at Five.

She gave me a smile I'd once taken as love.

The skin connecting her ear wasn't tight, but it wasn't loose, and then I realized she was purposefully relaxing her jaw and setting her teeth.

I was granted a Gift of Understanding. It was the most intense vision I'd ever experienced, not only a movie, but a montage with Elvis singing and changing scenery and the passage of time, and it was One and Five leaving us to go participate in The Day of Gifts and it was them fleeing, them not enacting change, them driving south. It was the Johnsons from Durango, wigs and fake IDs, reaching the border and then disappearing into sun-bleached

Mexico, and it was flashes of memory—the tickle of One's upper lip as he confessed into my ear, that tickle being the hints of stubble, stubble being something that shouldn't have existed in a man ingesting such high amounts of Cytoxan, and it was my hand running over Five's bare belly, her stomach feeling hard and full, which I'd believed to be constipation, but it wasn't, it was their chance at starting over again, amassing the things that had been ripped away by the world and cancer, a baby, a fucking baby—and it was them in Mexico and them sitting around a fire on the beach and them roasting marshmallows with their toddler and them a family, nuclear, happy, together.

One looked at me. He knelt down. He pressed his forehead to mine. I studied the whites of his eyes for Truth and I studied them for deceit and I realized I had never been able to tell the difference. He said, "None of this could have been possible without you. Thirty-Seven, you are The One. You are a Prophet. You are a visionary. Never forget that."

Those were the last words One ever spoke to me.

They walked out of the Greyhound station together, not holding hands, but close.

# 39. QUESTIONING

We're at Talley's Tatters and neither of us is sick because we've already been granted Truth. It's the first week of January. Snow falls.

The door opens.

Two cops walk in, a man and a woman.

My pulse is a double kick drum. Two greets them as they pretend to look around. I'm thinking about the DEA agents. I'm half expecting One to rush out from a hidden rack of clothes and take care of the complication. I tell myself nothing happens by accident. I tell myself I am above normal social interactions. I loosen my jaw and then set my teeth without clamping down.

"Elizabeth Smoltz?" one of the cops says.

Two nods. "Is there something I can help you with?"

"Oh, probably not," he says. "Slow day out there."

Two smiles. She rubs her bald head. The female cop walks toward me. I understand they will talk to us separately, but at the same time. I understand this is an initial feeling-out process. They will try to be our friends. They will wait for us to incriminate ourselves. I understand all of this because I am God.

"How's business?" she asks. She's the type of woman whose father loved her with all his heart but would've loved her more if she'd been a man.

"Slow season," I say.

"Nobody has any money left after Christmas," she says.

I smile and nod, but not too much as to appear desperate. The male cop speaks with Two. I can't hear what they're saying. I ask if she's looking for anything in particular.

"Oh, I don't think so. Just poking around."

She thinks she's clever. I know it's served her well over the years, her cleverness, her distrust, her eye for detail. It looks a lot like a life lived in Honesty, but she uses her intuitive powers to shield herself from Truth.

"Great," I say.

"Well, there is one thing," she says.

She looks at me. She says, "I'm sure it's nothing, but we're actually..." She leans forward like she's letting me in on a secret. I know this is to build a sense of trust. "We're actually following up on a homicide that occurred the other day."

"Around here?"

"Yeah, not too far."

"I'm not sure what I can do to help, but I'm all yours."

The cop stares at me. Her nostrils are wider than most Caucasians. She smiles. "Good. That's good. I'm glad you said that. Because I just have a few questions, then I'll be on my way."

"Of course."

"You see, there were a few people who saw some people around the scene of the crime who...well...matched your descriptions."

"Our descriptions?"

"Elizabeth Smoltz and Mason Hues. That's you, right?"

"That's me."

"Again," she said, leaning against the purple counter, "I'm sure it's nothing. Bald heads. Probably more common than they were in my day."

"Probably."

"But the crazy thing is, I was running the descriptions through our database, and your picture popped up. And there's a brand-new photo of you with that shiny noggin. I spoke with Officer Mack, and he informed me where you worked. We're probably grasping at straws, but you got to fill the day somehow, right?"

I nod.

I know it's not going to end.

This is the first.

They will send more.

They will keep coming because we're different and we're living a life dedicated to Honesty and they can sense this and it produces fear.

"Now, tell me, Mason, what was it you were incarcerated for as a juvenile?"

"I don't have to tell you that."

"No, no you don't. But I thought you said you wanted to help."

"I do. But I've given my adolescence to you, and my record is sealed in return. Now, if there's anything about this homicide I can help with…"

The cop smiles. She nods. She's going through the thought process of putting me in the category of suspect to prime suspect, a guilty boy who understands his basic rights.

"Of course," she says. "Fair is fair."

I look over her shoulder. Two's all smiles with the male cop. The female cop follows my gaze, turning around, then back to me.

"Just as a formality, can you tell me where you were on the morning of January first?"

I don't give her the satisfaction of pretending to think. I stare at her nostrils and then her skin connecting her ear and then her eyes. I tell her I was in our apartment.

"Oh, you two are a…"

"A what?"

"An item?"

"We don't put labels on things."

"Right. How *uncool* of me."

"No worries," I say.

"The whole night?"

"I'm sorry?"

"That whole night, you were in the apartment?"

"More or less."

"Tell me about the less."

"We went out."

"Where'd you go?"

"To help the homeless."

The cop's eyebrows rise. She nods like she's impressed. "That's mighty noble of you. Around here?"

"Yeah."

"Did you happen to venture down to the RINO district at all?"

"I don't think so."

"You don't think so?"

"That's what I just said."

The cop grins and taps the counter. She looks at my hand and then she looks back up to me and her cheekbones are more promi-nent than before and I know she's trying to contain excitement at her cleverness.

"What'd you do to your hand there?"

"Cut it."

"Looks pretty nasty. You get stiches?"

"Just hydrogen peroxide." I show her my palm and then I bring my hand to my side.

"How'd you get that cut?"

"A bottle."

"You know what they say," she says. "In the fight between man and bottle, the bottle always wins."

I stare through her. I smile. I think about my DNA being all over that Juggalo, and probably Two's as well from the ripping of her anus. I'm thinking about consequences being man-made and not real and I'm thinking of Truth being combustible, those in possession of it being consumed by its power. I know it's happening, has happened, will happen.

"Well, Mason, I really do appreciate your time."

"Let me know if there's anything else I can do to help."

She pauses. It's a dramatic effect learned from TV. She steps back to the counter. She says, "There's one last thing."

"Yup?"

"Why the shaved heads?"

"We like the look."

She nods. She says, "Yeah, you two don't really strike me as the skinhead type."

"Nope."

"Or even crazier, some Survivors wannabes."

"No, not that either."

I tell Two about the night One killed the DEA agents. I tell her everything because there are no secrets. I tell her how One gave a speech that night. How he told us it was over. How Truth couldn't be contained. How it consumed the vessels it traveled through. She asks what I'm saying. I tell her our lives in Denver have run their course. She nods. She presses against my chest. We're in our apartment and we're naked and we're covered in one another's fluids.

"You never talk about it," she says.

"What?"

"The Day of Gifts."

"What is there to say?"

"Who'd you kill?"

"I didn't."

Two props herself up on her elbow. Her small breasts brush against my chest. "You didn't?"

"I was supposed to, but I was too sick. I could hardly stand."

Two stares into my eyes. She's searching. We're all searching. She purses her lips, about to say something, but lies back down.

"Don't do that ever again," she says.

"Do what?"

"Lie to my face."

I feel like a failure and a phony. I take Two's hand. I tell her I'm sorry. She tells me to only apologize if I have no intention of ever repeating the same action. I apologize again.

"One gave me specific instructions. Everyone else's people were random, just cities and towns. But he told me who I was supposed to give my gift to."

"Who?"

"My mother."

"Like you were supposed to kill your father?"

"Yes."

"Jesus."

"Yeah."

We're quiet. Semen dries on my leg and itches. We know this will be the last night we spend on the mattress.

"And you couldn't do it?"

"I couldn't do it."

"He deserved it."

"We all deserve to die."

"But especially him."

"I let selfish fear overtake me."

"There are no accidents."

"Everything is an accident," I say.

"They will come back," Two says. "The cops. They won't stop until they pin it on us."

"I know."

"Do you ever think about it?"

"Huh?"

"If you'd killed your father?"

"Yes."

"I feel afraid."

"That's normal."

"I haven't felt this way in forever. Like not even when that motherfucker was raping me. Not like this."

"I thought it was all about fear," I say. "The One Truth."

"I fucking love you."

"We killed seventy-seven people. Nothing changed."

"Everything changed."

"You ask if I ever think about it, and I do. But you know the messed-up thing?"

"Huh?"

"I play the tape in my mind, and it always turns into me lying in bed with my dad in the doorway."

"Protection."

"Love."

"You're the most amazing person I've ever met," Two says.

"It wasn't supposed to end this quickly," I say.

"Nothing ever ends."

"Everything ends."

"Not for Gods."

"Especially for Gods."

"That's bullshit," Two says. "Everything you've ever done has af-
fected somebody. Everything. Like those guys we gave forgiveness
to. All the family members in the mountains. The Notes. And those
are just the big things. Like really fucking big. Like bigger than anyone can dream of. And me...I mean, fuck, man, you gave me life."

"We're going to be fugitives."

"I don't give a fuck. You hear me? You gave me the very thing
every human has ever searched for. You gave me God."

"I love you," I say.

"And love, baby, you gave me love."

"It's all the same."

"Because each of us is God. We can enact change through
whatever tool we want. We can give love or we can give fear or we
can give hope. I mean, that's what you all didn't grasp in Marble.
Each of us who possesses the One Truth can change the world
however the fuck he wants."

"I love listening to your Honesty."

Two straddles me. The lips of her vagina wrap around my penis's underbelly. She slowly rocks. She asks me about my first love. I
tell her about an amazing woman I met who offered me a job. I tell
her I was immediately drawn to her, both her sexy looks and her
seeking aura. Two grinds her pelvis. I tell her how I was all messed
up when I met this girl and wanted her to like me and was scared
of who I was because I had no idea. I tell her things changed with
forced Honesty. I say, "She forced me to quit living in selfish fear."
I'm hard again. I tell her that we built a loving family of our own
choosing. That we became sick together. That we saw our worst
and most vulnerable selves. That we loved with such ferocity we
didn't need to touch. I tell her we started changing the world. And
then we took a life because it was Honest. Two inches off of me,
sliding my penis inside of her. I tell her this girl took my virginity

and she was the most beautiful person in the world and that she was a prophet and a goddess and that she accomplished the impossible: enacting change through happiness.

Two rides me. Her eyes are soft orbs of vulnerability. She asks my favorite memory. I say, "This very second."

Two goes faster. She slams down on my hips. We are vessels of Truth. We are combustible. We know this and we race against our immolation and we want to consume one another and I love her so fucking much.

She pants, asking me my biggest regret.

I'm about to come and I buck and squeeze Two's flesh and she moans and bites her lip to the point of rupture and I tell her my biggest regret is that I didn't kill my father and then she comes and I come and we are nothing and everything and we understand what we're going to do without saying anything because we are a single mind.

# 40. TALKING

I made my first telephone call in close to a year.[11]

---

11 In *Dr. Sick: The Survivors and The Day of Gifts*, O'Connor reprints the entirety of my 911 call.

"911, what is your emergency?"
"People are going to die."
"Excuse me?"
"Dr. James Shepard is behind it."
"Sir, are you in danger?"
"We're all in danger."
"Where is your current location?"
"Truth."
"Sir, I need your name."
"Thirty-Seven."
"Your address? Thirty-seven *what*?"
"Gifts."

O'Connor breaks down the phone call. He dips into my head. He takes the liberties of presuming he knows what I was thinking. He writes, "Thirty-Seven, known simply as John Doe, the youngest member of The Survivors, experienced a moment of clarity. On some fundamental level, he understood what was about to transpire. He resisted Shepard's brainwashing. A germinating doubt blossomed into an attack of conscience...Thirty-Seven attempted to give his own form of gift on February tenth, and that gift was a warning."

O'Connor thinks this because I said as much when I was picked up three days later. I didn't talk and then I did and I told them whatever they wanted to know or maybe what I was willing to tell them.

They pushed and pushed and pushed for the whereabouts of the DEA agents.

I told them I had no idea what they were talking about.

I was held captive. I wasn't offered a lawyer, because of Homeland Security. I didn't care. I knew how to look people in the eye and project what they wanted to believe. I had no allegiances to One or Five because they'd sold us out for selfish wants.

And that was the real reason for the phone call. I wasn't thinking about sleeping families being awoken to puncture wounds. I wasn't thinking about accent walls being splattered with blood. I was thinking about One and Five in Mexico and them being happy and alone and with their new child that I wanted to be me. I was lamenting the fact we'd ever come back from Mexico. I was imagining that moment in the ocean as something permanent, something that didn't crush me. I was picturing the three of us—we'd grow hair and we'd live a simple life, and I'd learn to surf and I'd meet someone, a local girl with dark hair on her arms, and things would be quiet and we'd eat fruit and I'd speak various dialects of Truth and Romantic languages and it'd be a loving family of all of our choosing.

All of that, juxtaposed to the image of them leaving us at the Greyhound station, their hands so close to touching, magnetism.

Five was arrested in Sioux Falls, South Dakota. A family had been butchered seven hours before her incarceration. She was picked up walking along the highway. She wore her black scrubs even though it was only seventeen degrees. She was covered in blood. She didn't say anything. She didn't resist.

One was arrested in Oklahoma City. He was pulled over because he drove two missing DEA agents' car. He wore black scrubs. The previous night, the OKCPD had received four different calls, each parent hysteric, words failing, their children killed in the dark hours.

I didn't know this at the time, so I talked and I talked with varying levels of Honesty.

I acted out of jealousy.

I acted out of fear of being abandoned.

I acted out of my need for love.

Dr. Turner said everything stemmed from being given up for adoption. She said everything stemmed from my father pleasuring himself in my doorway. One said everything stemmed from our consciousness disconnect from God. He said that God wasn't real. He said everything came from humans knowing this Truth, but doing everything in their power—consuming and fucking and drinking and creating art and kneeling in mass and fighting wars and masturbating over our sleeping sons—to blot out this understanding, to live a life based in deceit. Two said that One's Truth was only a partial truth. She said that the One Truth is that we are Gods. Each of us. Everyone who has so much as screamed outside of his mother's womb. She said that armed with this knowledge, we can enact change through whatever tool we want.

I don't know, maybe they're all right.

O'Connor writes, "Thirty-Seven retreated from Glenwood Springs back up to Marble. He was in search of safety. He craved sanctuary. But upon arriving at Shepard's cabin, seeing it was still deserted, save for the ghosts of his fellow Survivors, who at that moment were in the process of murdering innocent people, he understood that this cabin, once a refuge, was now nothing more than a reminder of the atrocities he was complicit in…At that point, the only thing for a fifteen-year-old who'd been forced to undergo chemotherapy, forced to ingest highly disruptive hallucinogens, forced to offer up his body for any Survivor who felt a taste for youth, to do was to burn the house down. He had to destroy the physical representation of the mental hell he'd been enslaved to."

In CMHIP, I thought a lot about my willingness to abandon faith in One. I couldn't help but feel like Judas. I'd gotten scared, everything a Reprieve-like jumble of hurt. I'd allowed my sense of others, my intuition, my Gifts of Understanding, to skew. I'd seen what I wanted to see. I sold them out. I told things that shouldn't have been told. I agreed to deals. I craved intimacy. I became a mute. I became Mason Hues. I steeled my resolve in Dr. Turner's office, highlighting a book I practically wrote, seeing inconsistencies as facts, telling myself that One and Five might have participated in The Day of Gifts, but they were still running away together as the Johnsons from Durango. I did this and I became happier or at least not suicidal. I didn't think about Truth. I didn't think about Honesty. I masturbated to fantasies other than One or my father. I played four square in the rec room. I never used the first person plural. I was given small rewards: extra pudding, promises to not go back to juvie, the ability to keep *Dr. Sick* in my room. I blotted out everything I'd learned and I talked about being a victim and I wrote letters we burned and I believed Dr. Turner when she said I could be anything I wanted to.

And then I was given a Gift of Understanding.

Sometimes I wonder why I didn't simply tell them all where the DEA agents were buried.

I suppose it's because that's where I went after I burned the cabin down. I walked seven miles into the mountains. I climbed up to the abandoned quarry. I sat above the quartered bodies and I shivered and I cried and I prayed for death. I spoke to voices that echoed up fifty feet, the words muffled through two Hefty trash bags. They told me they loved me. They told me nothing was my fault. They told me One and Five had abandoned the Honest life months before. They told me my family members were changing the world the best way they knew how. They told me I was pretty. That someday I'd make somebody happy. They told me nothing happened by accident. They told me they'd always be there for me. They weren't mad. They were happy I was born. They were proud of me.

None of this is in the book.

Instead, O'Connor paints a picture of me stumbling through the woods for three days. He engages in every sensationalized bit of bullshit he can muster. I know this is his attempt to paint me as sympathetic. To illustrate how I may have been involved in monstrous things, but I was fifteen; I was not a monster. He writes about hypothermia and starvation, a lonely boy in need of rescue. He writes, "After seventy hours, Thirty-Seven's body failed him. He crumpled to the snow. He was two hundred yards from the cabin, close enough to feel its magnetism, far enough away to protect himself from its deadly grasp."

# 41. GHOSTS

We have two notes to leave: one for Henry O'Connor, one for Dr. Turner.

We drive across the flats of our country in eleven hours. In Nebraska, Two asks if I want to try driving and I tell her *no* and she tells me I'm the worst liar she's ever met. We switch seats. I practice in a Walmart parking lot. I drive on the highway and even get the car up to seventy-five.

Henry O'Connor is old so he lists his phone number and address in the white pages. He lives on Summit Avenue. We arrive in St. Paul, Minnesota, at eight in the morning. The town is cute in the way the Midwest is cute with snow and people bundled up and the notion of trudging. We stop in front of his house. It's an old Victorian with three overgrown evergreens in the yard and ornate shingles in the shape of tears.

It's cold without the heater running. I hold Two's hand. She says, "Now what?"

"We get seen."

Henry O'Connor is fatter in person than on the back of *Dr. Sick*. He waddles out of his house after we've been waiting for an hour.

He climbs into a black BMW. He backs down his fifty-foot drive-way. He struggles to crane his neck around for oncoming traffic, then rights his car and starts down Summit. O'Connor turns as he passes our parked car. He looks at two people with no hair. We pull out and follow.

He turns onto Grand Avenue. People walk into bakeries and people are happy even though it's only fifteen degrees. Two tells me the roads are icy and I tell her she's doing well. We follow O'Connor four blocks to a Starbucks. He pulls into the small lot. We drive up a little ways and park. O'Connor gets out. He looks around, prob-ably for us. He goes inside. He comes out ten minutes later. He merges into the crawling traffic and then he is at our side and he sees us and we stare with Honesty and Truth. I'm granted a Gift of Understanding—O'Connor and his wife sitting around an oak din-ing table, his wife trying her best to show excitement while voicing her concern about the publication of a book about a murderous cult, O'Connor placing his meaty hand over his wife's, telling her she has nothing to fear, every single member of The Survivors was either dead or in prison, and here he smiles, mostly for his wife's benefit, but partially for his own reassurance.

We follow the black BMW for another mile. The age of people tromping through the snow lowers. They wear skinnier jeans and longer coats. We see a sign for Macalester College, where O'Connor teaches. He pulls into a parking lot and we keep going and find street parking a block up. Before we get out of the car, Two puts her forehead to mine. She says, "Thank you."

"For what?"

"Everything."

The air is freezing on my bald head. Little shards of ice blow. My lungs feel mentholated. We hold hands walking down the street. A middle-aged woman with a red turtleneck underneath a parka looks at us and then our heads and then us again and she smiles with empathy because she thinks we're sick.

We walk through the campus. It's small, the buildings seventies style with concrete and darkened windows. The sky has a lot of gravity. We step inside of the student union. Artsy kids and Asians sit at tables with textbooks open. I think about being one of these kids. I think about college. Dr. Turner was always pushing me to go. She was always telling me I could be anything I wanted. I think it's weird that One never told me that, only that I would change the world. I think about it no longer mattering, or maybe it never mattered. There are no accidents. I'd seen Dr. Turner's Truth, which jolted me back to a life dedicated to Honesty.

We make our way to the history building. We walk through the halls. We are a college couple in love and stressed with our heavy course loads. We find Henry O'Connor's office. The door is closed. He has a Peanuts cartoon taped underneath his nameplate. We wait at the end of the hallway. Two is excited. She keeps glancing back to O'Connor's office. I tell her I love her and she smiles. She asks me what I'm thinking about. I tell her going to college. She says it sucks unless you're into date rape and student debt.

"Besides," she says, "who can teach you anything?"

"Pretty much anyone."

"That's why it had to be you," she says.

"Why what had to be me?"

"The One who actually enacts change."

We hear the door open. A chubby coed dressed in too-tight leggings walks out. O'Connor follows. He glances in our direction and we don't flinch or even blink. He stares. We're holding our coats so our black scrubs are visible. He walks with the girl in the opposite direction. When he turns the corner, he sneaks a final peek back. I

can't see his pupils, but I know they're dilated in his body's prepara-
tion to flee.

We wait for O'Connor's class to end. All of the students file out.
Two takes my hand and we walk into the lecture hall. It's smaller
than I'd seen in movies, four tiers of ten-person tables and a smart
board. O'Connor stands at the podium. He seems like the type of
man to lecture from a podium; I bet it comes across as preaching.

O'Connor pushes his glasses in with his index finger. He looks
around the room and then back at us. He clears his throat. He says,
"May I help you?"

We stare down at a man who has profited off of my life. A
man who has taken my story and sensationalized it, spun it to be
about Reprieve and sex, about murder, about Dr. James Shepard
and Cytoxan and premeditation. He feared what we'd done in the
mountains. He feared it because it was about change and he feared
it because it lifted the veil of the One Truth every person knows
but won't allow themselves to feel. So he'd discredited everything.
He'd packaged it for Hollywood. He'd dumbed it down for Middle
American families who needed to believe in Good versus Evil.

We don't say anything.

"I asked if I can help you," O'Connor says. He starts fussing
with a few papers. He stacks them against the podium and slips
them in his leather briefcase. He takes a few steps, and then real-
izes he shouldn't turn his gaze from us. His next steps are cautious.

"These rooms have cameras," he says. He points to the ceiling.
We don't look. He shakes his head like the whole thing is juvenile.
"I don't know who you two are, but I know you've been following
me. I know this stunt is harassment. If it persists, I will have you
two arrested."

He expects us to be scared.

He pulls out a phone from his pocket. He waves it like a weapon. He walks to the far side of the room and then starts up the steps. He says, "Last chance." We don't move. He shakes his head and punches in a few numbers. He puts his phone to his ear. His breathing is an asthma attack. He stands on our level. He tries so hard not to show fear. He speaks into his phone: "I'd like to report physical harassment. Two people have been following me and now have attempted to corner me in a classroom...Macalester College...Yes, they have threatened me."

He puts the phone against his lapel. He says, "They are dispatching units this instant."

I know he's lying because he hasn't told them which building he's in and because the mere act of calling the police would make this experience real, and he's not willing to go there, at least not yet.

"Hope this stunt was worth it," O'Connor says.

He walks to the exit on the opposite side of the landing. He pushes open the door. His proximity to the exit gives him courage. "There is nothing more pathetic than a copycat."

We wait for night to fall, which comes early being this far north. We watch lights turn on throughout O'Connor's house. We see shapes through curtain-drawn windows. We imagine them eating. We are hungry, so we split a Mr. Pibb. We don't take our ipecac because we've already arrived at Truth.

We shiver and hold hands.

We watch the downstairs lights turn off. We trace bodies through walls. The bedroom lights turn on and then the bathroom. Twenty minutes later, the lights reverse their order. Two lamps, his and hers.

At ten, one lamps turns off.

Fifteen minutes later, the other lamp cuts.

We wait a half hour and then get out of the car. The temperature has to be in the single digits. We walk up the driveway and
then around the back of the house. A security system decal is plastered to the glass on the back door. This is expected. We'd written
the note beforehand.

Two looks at me and I nod but this isn't what she wants. She
presses her head to mine. I press back. She says, "I love you so fucking much."

"More than anything that will ever exist," I say.

Two smashes a rock through the glass. Sirens sound immediately. She reaches through and unlocks the door and she says *shit*
and then *fuck* and she brings her arm back out of the broken window. Her hand bleeds. She opens the door. We walk inside. We walk
across the kitchen. We stick our note on the refrigerator. We hear
heavy footsteps coming down the stairs and then we are running
outside and then down the driveway and we are in the car pulling
away by the time the downstairs lights are on.

We drive down Summit Avenue. We get on I-94 West. Two
drives the speed limit. She holds her hand in her lap. Blood pools
against her coat. I look at my own hand, the jagged slice from stab-
bing the Juggalo. I run my nail against the crusty scab. I'm bleeding.
I reach over and take Two's hand. She understands I want all of her
inside of me. She smiles because we want to be the same deity. She
starts laughing. I don't need to ask what's funny because I know
everything is funny because it doesn't matter and because we are
blood brothers and because we are enacting change and because we
are combusting with Truth and because we're in love and then her
laughs turn to ecstatic screams and she lets go of my hand and slams
her bleeding hand on the steering wheel and I join in and there is
nothing besides our screams and the ghosts of our pasts and that
very moment.

# 42. PUEBLO

We drive back to Colorado, but we don't stop in Denver because that part of our lives is over with. We head to Pueblo. It's early afternoon. We find a Motel 6 for $59 a night. We unpack and lie on a bed with a box spring. We watch HBO until it gets dark and then we drive toward the south end of town.

We approach the CMHIP. It's smaller than I remember, a concrete block halfheartedly dressed up with Doric columns. The parking lot is dark and mostly empty. The front of the building is lit with spotlights. I count over three windows on the third floor. I imagine looking out of those locked windows and praying for something to change. Two backs into a parking spot that affords us a view of the entire lot. It's Thursday, and Dr. Turner always worked the second shift on Thursdays. We'll see her leave. We'll follow her home. We'll leave a note stating we could've killed her, but instead gave her a gift.

Two asks what's going on inside my beautiful head.

I speak with Honesty because that's all I know. "I want to go in."

"Like to visit?"

"To live."

"Safety," Two says.

"I guess," I say.

"Makes sense," Two says. "But that doctor…"

"Is consumed with selfish wants."

Two says, "I was going to say is a fucking cunt, but, yeah."

I smile. I say, "It's all so malleable."

"What is?"

"The mind."

"Until you arrive at Truth."

"Even then," I say. "Doubt, fear, need for love."

"You don't see it," Two says. "How fucking amazing you are."

"I'd given up on One inside of those walls. That's the real Truth. Completely given up, believed everything in O'Connor's book, everything Dr. Turner told me."

"Because they systematically broke you down," Two says.

"A loose and broad narrative."

"All those meds they had you on, locked rooms, *revoked privileges*…of course you believed what they told you."

"Cytoxan and Reprieve."

Two shakes her head. She says, "There are no accidents. None. You had to undergo both places to arrive here. To arrive at Truth. To meet me. To change the fucking world."

A woman walks out of the front doors. She's thin. She pulls a knee-length parka tightly across her chest. I can't see her face, but I don't need to. Dr. Turner walks to her Land Rover. She climbs inside the car. Two doesn't say anything, just puts the car in drive.

We follow Dr. Turner for fifteen minutes. We climb foothills. Houses become nicer and more secluded. I hold Two's hand, but we don't press with any force. Dr. Turner turns into a driveway that looks more like a road. Her car disappears into trees and darkness. We park.

We sit there. The car becomes cold. Our breaths remind us we're alive because they steam the windows. Two says she misses getting sick and I tell her I know what she means. She asks if it was weird seeing Dr. Turner. I shake my head, but then say, "Kind of."

"I bet."

"The matriarch of that whole place. Part therapist, part ward mother."

"She have kids?"

"Don't think so."

"It's weird," Two says.

"What?"

"How people in positions of power always betray."

"How'd your parents betray you?"

"Gave me everything I wanted."

I nod. I respect her Honesty. I respect her insight.

"This is it," I say. "We leave this note..."

"It's already over," Two says.

"Do you think about what it's like to die?"

"Better than prison," Two says.

"No, I'm serious."

"So am I."

"To cease to exist. Nothing. One minute, you're thinking, the next minute—"

"You're free," Two says.

"Of suffering?"

"Of everything."


We wait for an hour and then get out of the car. We're dressed in our scrubs. Our bare arms are littered with goose bumps. An owl calls. We walk down a twisty driveway. The house is big and expensive, modern with flat surfaces and oddly placed rectangular windows. I have the note tucked into the waistband of my pants. We are leaving notes and we are enacting change the way it needs to be enacted with people like O'Connor and Dr. Turner, who believe Truths can be printed in books and people's worldviews can be systematically eradicated through talking about childhoods and sexual desires. We are giving them gifts. It will be different with my father—his chance for redemption has come and gone. That gift will go to my mother.

The front door is orange. We walk around to the back. We test sliding-glass doors and then the garage and this door opens. We walk inside. My heart pounds because I am nothing but Truth. I put my hand on the chrome handle leading inside of the house. It turns. We're inside. There's no alarm because people like Dr. Turner don't believe in monsters.

We step into her kitchen. It's beautiful—white on white, quartz counters, everything planned and everything perfect—and I imagine Dr. Turner choosing these counters, poring over modern architecture magazines, dog-earing pages, so happy with herself, so happy with the notion of Perfect Home, so delusional to think this would cure a goddamn thing.

I'm walking over to the stainless-steel refrigerator when I hear nails against hard wood. Then there's a dog, a Husky, and it's barking, loud barks that are rooted in fear and are more Honest than anything I've ever heard.

The door we walked through closes behind Two. It isn't loud, but the sound's enough to set the dog off. It lunges from its stance, past me, toward Two. The dog jumps and then Two screams and they're on the floor and the screaming escalates and I'm nothing but reaction, grabbing a sauté pan from the wrought-iron rack hanging above the island. I rush toward Two. The Husky has Two pinned. Its jaw is clamped around her arm. I raise the pan and I'm thinking about a poodle I was too scared to kill and about there being no accidents and about the certain failure of anyone attempting to recreate a past experience. I make contact with the dog's head. It lets out a screeching cry. I hit it again and again and again.

Two's covered in blood. I don't know if it's her blood or the dog's. I don't know if it matters.

"Don't move."

I spin around. Dr. Turner stands there in panties and a cami and her arms are outstretched and they shake and they hold a revolver.

We lock eyes. I'm granted a Gift of Understanding. It's Dr. Turner in her late teens and she's in love with the world and with the notion of college and she's walking to her car at the mall and there's an attack and there's penetration and there's the smell of onions on the attacker's breath and there's promises of death and there's him forcing her to open her mouth and then there's his phlegm in her mouth. He has become a piece of her. She keeps good on her promise. She keeps her mouth shut. She quits walking alone at night. She becomes involved with Take Back the Night. She learns to shoot a gun from one of her graduate school friends. She holds people at distance, more men than women, but both. She wants to know why this man attacked her. She wants to know the kind of broken that forces itself inside of another. She wants to learn to fix him so she can fix herself. She's had a gun for the majority of her adult life. She knows how to shoot it. She will feel no remorse, but rather a tremendous sense of relief, me dying the death of her attacker.

I hold up my hands.

"Mason?"

"Dr. Turner."

"What…Jesus Christ."

She looks down at the black and white clump of dog on the floor. Tears start. Two pulls herself around the far side of the island counter.

"What have you done?"

I don't answer because it's obvious.

"Mason, do you...what have...do you realize what they'll...*why*?"

"It attacked me."

Dr. Turner chokes out a sob. Her knees are skinny and they shake. She wipes the back of her hands against her nose and then trains the gun on me. My hands are still up. I feel the dog's blood against my shoes. I will not beg for my life because it doesn't matter or maybe I will not beg for my life because I can see the Honesty of Dr. Turner's whites, and there isn't death there, only regret.

"Why?"

"I was going to leave you a note."

She lets out another sob.

"You're not Thirty-Seven, Mason. You're not that person. You're past that. We got you past that. What the...Jesus, your hair."

Dr. Turner's shaking; she's afraid. But it's pity she's crying over. Pity for me. Pity for herself and her failures. Pity for the Truth that people don't change; they learn to hide detestable traits until their sons are asleep and they can masturbate over sleeping bodies in peace. I see Two rising from the far side of the island. I stare at Dr. Turner. I say, "You said I could do anything I wanted. Be anyone I wanted."

Dr. Turner leans forward as if infused with physical pain. I think about family members doubling over paint buckets. The gun lowers. She stares at me and then her dead dog and then back at me. The skin connecting her ear fluctuates between taut and loose. Two is a shadow and she's invisible and she's the most beautiful thing I've ever seen and everything is a repetition of everything else and she raises her hand holding the metal pan and she's One raising his gun to the DEA agents' heads and the only thing I want to say is *I love you more than you love me.*

Two swings the pan against Dr. Turner's head.

Dr. Turner drops.

I want to tell her to stop, but I don't because there are no accidents.

Two bashes until there's nothing left.

I imagine One doing the same to Thirty-Eight. I imagine the loving family of my own choosing doing the same to seventy-seven innocent people. I imagine myself doing it to the piece of shit raping Two. I imagine doing it to my father. Everything ends in death—this is the One Truth—and Two stands over a dead body and she turns and her pale face is splattered with blood. She walks across the wooden floor. We press our heads together. Both are slick. Things taste metallic. We are so close to combusting and we are Truth and we are God and we are one.

# 43. FAMILIES OF ORIGIN[12]

---

12 Henry O'Connor has a chapter in *Dr. Sick* titled "Families of Origin." It's one of two told in mosaic form (the other being the chapter "The Day of Gifts"). It is twenty-two hundred words, thirty-eight sections long. These sections are snippets of biographic information of each of us. They read somewhat like lists and somewhat like obituaries. It's the saddest chapter in the book.

The thirty-seventh section of "Families of Origin" is about me. It's obtuse because my identity is classified. O'Connor writes, "John Doe, aka Thirty-Seven, was fifteen years old when he joined The Survivors. The particulars of his upbringing are unknown, but one can safely assume his home life left much to be desired. He was too young for a driver's license. He was a freshman in high school. He was eighty-nine pounds when apprehended."

O'Connor strikes similar emotional chords with each member of my family. His writing is flat. He uses very few adverbs. He gives facts that come across as the most human thing in the book.

Vignette after vignette, we are chronicled.

Each of us is different, but each of us is the same.

We all lost someone or something or everyone or everything.

Cancer took most of our loved ones.

Abuse destroyed our psyches.

Some died in car accidents.

Some died because they put guns inside of their mouths.

O'Connor doesn't offer any insight in this particular chapter, which I applaud. It works better as an impression. The reader, even though he's hell-bent on understanding in order to gain a sense of control in order to keep fear at bay in order to preserve the fantasy of immortality in order to blot out the Truth that he, in fact, is the God he prays to for protection and love and raises at work and healthy children, can still pause, reflect, see us as human. The reader can deduce that his own family of origin wasn't as bad. Or if it was, he can feel good about the fact he didn't subject himself to round after round of chemotherapy and then break into strangers' houses and murder their families. The reader understands that we were looking for a new family. A new start. A new doctrine to live by. O'Connor uses the phrase "a loving family of his/her/ our choosing" twenty-seven times in *Dr. Sick*. Because that's what we sought. That's what we created. Really, it's as simple as that.

"Sasha Stein, aka Five, was born and raised in Fort Collins, Colorado. She was one of three children. She married when she was twenty. She became a nurse. She volunteered at her synagogue and she gave blood quarterly. A coworker, Shelly O'Rourke, described her as 'the most giving human I've ever met.' In 2009, her husband of eleven years died of prostate cancer. Both Sasha and her husband had lost their jobs the previous month. Sasha Stein was widowed and owed the hospital over two hundred thousand dollars."

I'd not known Five was Jewish.

I'd not known Eleven was a Gulf War vet.

I'd not known Twenty-Four had served five years in the penitentiary for possession with intent to distribute.

I'd not known One had been raised in a two-million-dollar condo in Manhattan.

One always said that we were not our pasts. He said we were not our differences. He said we were people dedicated to living Honestly among a loving family of our own choosing.

I think about the million people who've read *Dr. Sick: The Survivors and The Day of Gifts*. I think about them having a morsel of empathy. I wonder if they do what their religions preach: see themselves in somebody else's shoes. Dr. Turner was the first one to bring up this notion. We sat in her office. She asked me why I was crying. I didn't know because I was far from Honesty. I told her it wasn't supposed to be like that.

"Be like what, Mason?"

"Murder."

"What was it supposed to be like?"

"Love. Community. Family."

She nodded. She crossed her legs and I thought about running my hand up her thigh and then about Jerome and then about my father.

"But why are you *sad*?" she asked.

"Because they had no choice."

"People always have a choice."

"Not when there are no accidents."

"It sounds like you are speaking about *powerlessness*."

I nodded.

"What, in your *own* life, do you feel powerless over?"

"Everything."

"Like?"

"When I eat and sleep and what I do and what I watch—"

Dr. Turner held up her hand. She said, "What about *before* you arrived here?"

I thought for a minute. I wanted to say anything but my father. "My father."

Dr. Turner smoothed out her skirt. The skin connecting her ear tightened, but not in an aggressive way, more like she had an idea. She said, "Could it be that you, like The Survivors, experienced a powerlessness so absolute that violence felt like the only option?"

I conceded with a shrug.

"And perhaps, you're drawn to The Survivors because of this similarity?"

"I was drawn to them because we created a loving family of our own choosing out of shit. Out of death. Out of betrayal. Out of—"

"Abuse?"

"Yeah."

"Acceptance," Dr. Turner said. "It always comes back to acceptance. How to find it, where to find it, how to achieve it of our own actions."

"We had no choice," I said.

"You're exercising *empathy*," Dr. Turner said. "The ability to understand and share the feelings of another. This is good. This is really good."

I stared at Dr. Turner like she was an idiot. I said, "Isn't everybody who reads this book able to do the same?"

She shook her head. She said, "Not to the same levels, Mason."

# 44. HOME

We drive the speed limit. It's 11 a.m. and then it's 12 a.m. and then it's a new day. I haven't been back to Boulder since the night I ran away. It's grown. The Flatirons are like nestled clouds. I'm behind the wheel because Two bleeds from her hand and her arm and her chest. I think about my father teaching me to drive. I wonder if he'd have been patient. I wonder if he'd have told me I was doing a good job.

We're quiet. The adrenaline has subsided. We are alone in our thoughts of murder and what happens afterward. When we feel selfish want and fear creep back up, we squeeze one another's hands.

I drive through town.

Everything is a memory, none of them horrible, none of them happy. I turn on Broadway. A homeless man stares at me and I know he's a Seeker. I use the blinker. Two whimpers whenever she moves her right arm or really whenever she moves at all. I turn on Yale. I drive a block and then pull over. I bump the curb because the whole thing is new to me.

"This it?"

I don't respond. I feel Two's stare. She turns to her window. We look at a million-dollar bungalow with a porch swing. I stare into the attic window. I wonder if they've kept my room the same or made it into a study that's never used. I feel physically sick. It's not because of what we did to Dr. Turner and it's not because of what I'm about to give. It's because I am making good on an edict I abandoned. I'd lost Trust. I'd lost Truth. I'd lost Honesty. I'd betrayed everything I'd worked so hard to achieve because I was jealous and I was scared and I wanted to believe people were bad and selfish and capable of loving one another but not me. I think about it being different, The Day of Gifts, had I not phoned the police. I wonder if my family members would still be alive, or at least not incarcerated. Probably. I wonder if they would've dispersed and assimilated and become their dead loved ones, or if they'd have stayed dedicated to living an Honest life.

Two reads my mind because her blood courses through my veins and because we are nothing but conduits. She says, "There are no accidents. You did what you did. This is a chance for redemption. You have the opportunity to deliver a gift that your mother—no, fuck that, *the world*—needs to receive."

I nod.

"You have the opportunity that nobody else gets." Two reaches out and takes hold of my chin so I meet the whites of her eyes. "To erase your biggest regret. And in doing so, you will erase who you were. You'll erase Mason Hues. Thirty-Seven. All of it, gone. You will be One. You will no longer be tethered to this world. You will be free of Self."

I've never thought about this. I'm nodding. She leans forward. We press our foreheads. We kiss. My limbs find themselves with tingling pinpricks.

We stop kissing. Two speaks into my mouth: "Are you ready for us to change the world?"

I shake my head. "I'll go."

Two's whites search for Honesty. They find it. She nods and tells me she understands. I reach out and take the door handle. I pause. I ask if she has her phone.

"Yeah, why?"

"Do you have any Elvis?"

Two smiles. She scrolls through her library. Her fingers leave bloody streaks. She shakes her head and tells me she has a cover of "Blue Moon," but that's it. I tell her that works. She finds a pair of earbuds in the glove box. She tells me to be careful and to be Honest and I say, "I love you so fucking much."

I get out of the car. It's cold and windy and everything feels fake. I'm fifteen and I'm coming home from school and I'm hoping my father isn't home and I'm hoping he is. I'm fifteen and I'm dressed in black scrubs and I'm doing my part in The Day of Gifts. I'm eighteen and I'm probably wanted for murder and I know I will die and part of me doesn't want it to end because I have someone to share it with.

I walk to the front door. I kick away snow, searching for the fake rock containing a key. I can't find it. I walk around the side of the house. I run my hands over windows. I walk to the back. I stand in my childhood yard. I'm learning to cast a fly rod. I'm eating burgers. I'm sitting in a baby pool staring at people I think will never hurt me.

I break the glass with a rock.

I wait for sounds, for lights, for alarms.

Nothing.

I arrange the earbuds. I press *play*. A slow, country version of "Blue Moon" comes on. The woman's voice sounds like sickness and beauty. My steps are silent. I am a ghost. I am a demon. I am a giver of gifts. I slide the largest knife out from the wooden block. I'm thinking about lying on carpet while vomiting and shitting my pants and I'm thinking about lying in bed pretending to be asleep and I'm thinking everything happens for a reason and Two came into my life to lead me to Truths I was too young and scared and broken to accept the first time around.

The stairs don't squeak because I know where to step.

The pictures of me along the staircase have been removed. Instead, my parents smile like they are happy and did a good job with parenthood, or maybe those smiles are real and they feel blessed to be done with me.

I'm my father walking down the hallway. I'm slightly drunk and certain the rest of the family is asleep. I feel like I've done well that day, been a good father, a good husband, even got in a bike ride. I feel like I deserve this. And who's it even hurting? Mason should be thanking *me* I don't enact the same things that were done to me by my father. I'm a saint to keep these urges to his doorway. A fucking saint.

My mother and father are asleep. The cable's off but the TV's still on and things are electric gray. I am nothing. I have no weight or presence. Consciousness is a disconnect from God. We are God. Consciousness is a disconnect from ourselves. I stand at the foot of their bed. My mother faces the wall because even in her sleep, she knows the Truth about my father. My dad faces the ceiling. His mouth is open. I walk to his side. I stare at him. He looks older but still attractive, the lines of days-lived thicker, distinguished. The sides of his head have grayed. I watch his Adam's apple chug up and down as he swallows. I reach underneath the waistband of my scrubs. It only takes the act to get hard. I watch my father. I wonder what he's dreaming about. I wonder if he misses me. I wonder if he's glad I'm gone and I wonder if he's sad and I wonder if his biggest regret is what he did in the darkness of my room or if it's that he didn't do more. I go faster. I listen to a woman pay tribute to Elvis. Her voice is haunting. I think about my father waking up and him smiling, a dream come true. I wonder why my mother never did anything. She knew, just like anybody knows what goes on under the veil of suburban tranquility. I bite my lip. I don't care if the slapping sound wakes them up. I don't care about a single fucking thing and I've always cared about everything and I still do. I think about my birth mother. And I am granted a Gift of Understanding, my mother not a junkie or a thirteen-year-old victim of incest, but a housewife, mother of three, older, happy, just not wanting to do it all over again. I am the sacrificial lamb. I cry. I beg Jerome to hold me. I shiver on a boulder and whisper into One's ear and the euphoria I feel is life without the weight of a soul.

My eyes fall from my father's throat to his chest. That's when I see a thick red line dissecting his pectoral, the only bare patch on his chest. It's a scar. It's new. But not that new, the skin rounded and smooth. I see the tip of another scar at the base of his sternum. I use the tip of the knife to lower the silk sheets. His entire torso is covered in scars, easily ten, twelve, fifteen. Each one is around two inches in length. The knife hovers above his navel. I realize it's the same size as the scars.

I'm thinking about cancer and operations and car accidents. I'm masturbating over his sleeping body. I'm my father. I'm agreeing to adoption and I'm secretly excited about it being a boy. I'm terrified about when my son matures, adolescence shedding with the first definition of muscle. I want to watch him shower. I want to love him the way I was loved. I want to be immortal. I want to be loved. I want to be God.

Everything goes black and my body is nothing but the release of energy. The lyrics beg to be kept from harm. I pull up my pants. I lean over and kiss my father's forehead. I want this moment to last forever; I want this moment to be my happily ever after. I walk out of his life for a second time.

———

I walk back to the car. Two sees me. The door opens. She's crying and searching and I stare at her and then I lose it because I don't understand what the fuck is going on and she thinks I've killed him and I close my eyes so she keeps this belief. We don't press foreheads. We hug. We hug so hard. We cry. She tells me she's proud and that she loves me and that there are no accidents. I just keep sobbing. She says, "Shh, baby, shh. Everything's okay. You're okay. You're loved. You're safe."

I sob into her neck.

"Shh, baby, shh, you're with me now. I'm not going to let anyone hurt you."

# 45. TWO'S GIFT

It's close to five in the morning. We're in the mountains of Marble. I drive slowly by my former home. I keep going. I drive seven miles and then I pull over and park. Two doesn't ask where we're going because she knows or doesn't care. We bundle in our coats. We don't have the right kind of boots. The snow swallows our legs. Two bleeds. We hike. I can't stop picturing Dr. Turner's head, how flat it became underneath Two's Honesty. Same with my father. I don't know why I didn't killed him. I don't know why he was incapable of loving me how I needed to be loved.

The darkness hints at light.

It's going to be morning soon. People will climb out of beds and children will pretend to brush their teeth and people will complain about going to work while it's still dark. People will buy coffee. People will wait to go to the bathroom until they are on the clock. College kids will smile like they're in control of everything. Old people will walk to their television sets wearing the same thing they slept in. My mother will go to Pilates. She'll complain about feeling too busy. My father will read *The Washington Post* and feel smarter than any Republican. And when they are all doing these things, they will be thinking of something else, something they want to do or need to do, dinners that need to be prepared and dry cleaning that needs to be picked up and children that need to be bathed. And when they return home, they'll pretend to be excited. They'll feign gratitude at a family of their own choosing. They will masturbate in the shower. They will sneak nips of vodka in the pantry. They will watch their husband of fifty years snore in his chair and be struck with the crippling notion of wanting him dead and never loving someone so much, even her children.

Day after day.

Year after year.

This is what the American dream has always looked like.

Every single action is a stepping stool to another. Every conversation is one-sided, a mirror reflecting looks and status and wealth. Every person is steeped in want, and this is applauded. It's aptitude. It's go-get-'er-ness. It's hunger. It's filling themselves with goods and sex and alcohol and validation so they forget about the fact that they all will die. That there's no heaven. There's no reincarnation. There's nothing. Because Gods roam this earth, eight billion of them and counting. We all are God. We all have unlimited power and we all can access Truth through sickness and Honesty and we can see flashes of any past we desire to understand and we can move through the world like shadows.

I imagine an America in which this Truth is achieved.

This image fades into flames because Truth is shy and Americans are still Americans, each of us wanting to be a bigger God than our counterparts.

I wonder if we have enacted change.

I doubt it.

We could do the same thing every night for a year and still be cuckolded by denial.

Why?

Because the vast majority simply don't give a fuck about Honesty. They don't care about Truth. They want certainty. They want to believe the interns at the office are interested rather than nervous. They want their kids to be extensions of themselves. They want their house to be both a manifestation of their inadequate genitalia and a fortress to keep out the scary. They want to believe they are inherently different than everyone else, better.

I know this because I've experienced every single thing that has happened or will happen. I know this because I want a box spring. I know this because I would trade all the Truth in the world for my father to have read me stories instead of pleasuring himself in my doorway.

But that does not mean what we are doing is any less important. In fact, it's the opposite. Seekers will seek. Those who hunger and thirst for righteousness will grow tired of the church and start asking the right questions. Loved ones will die. Wives will cheat. Children will run away. And Two and I will be everyone at once. We will offer forgiveness. We will cause terror. We will force introspection. We will multiply. Sarah, the homeless girl who stole my computer, she's already turning. She'll spread our message. She won't know how or why she's doing it, but she'll understand when somebody is ready, and she'll lower her head, tell him to press his lips to her ear, and she'll ask about his first love, his favorite memory, and his biggest regret. He'll tell her. Souls will be exchanged. Self will become nonexistent, if only for a fraction of time. They will both feel it, the One Truth, that they're Gods, that anything is possible, that there are no accidents, that nothing matters and everything matters, that all anybody has ever wanted was love from a family of his own choosing.

The cave housing the abandoned mine shaft is exactly where I remember it to be. I stand behind Two. I help her when she slips. We're shivering. Two's dying. We pull ourselves to a small ledge.

Two rests against the granite. I'm crouched down, heading for the back. Only, the cave doesn't go back but a few feet. I run my hands against the rock. I look down, expecting to be standing over the metal grates covering the fifty-foot hole where we'd dropped the quartered bodies of the DEA agents. But there's nothing there. It has to be the wrong cave. I could've sworn it was where I'd come twice before, but there's no way.

"Baby," Two says.

I turn around. I walk the few steps to the cave's mouth. Two's looking at the rock wall. She runs her fingers over something. She says it's beautiful. I ask her what she's talking about.

"Your name."

I peer closer. MASON HUES is scratched into the rock. I don't remember doing this.

"10/24/12," Two says.

"What?"

"The date."

She points underneath my name. She turns, smiling. Her skin is so pale. I know she is nearly combusted. I can't go back to cooking rice alone. Her smile fades. She looks at the carving and then back at me. Her eyes are different, hooded.

"Why'd you put the wrong date?"

"What? I don't…"

"Because it would've been February tenth. The eleventh at the latest, right? That's when you were here, after The Day of Gifts."

I don't know what to say.

"But October twenty-fourth? That would've been—"

"The day I ran away," I say.

"So you came here first?"

I'm shaking my head or maybe my whole body is shaking. I step backward. My foot kicks something that rattles. I look down.

I'm stepping on a chopping knife. I bend over. I pick it up. The tip is dull, broken. I'd carved my name in the rock with it. That meant I'd brought it with me. And it'd been the day I'd run away from home. I'm thinking about having come here first instead of One's cabin. And it had to be a different cave than the one we'd dumped the bodies in and I'd later hid in for three days. Maybe I'd gotten confused and led us to the wrong one.

I hold the knife. I look down at Two. She isn't present, just a body and a mind. The skin connecting her ear pulls tight. The whites of her eyes are a television screen. And I'm inside of her mind, experiencing her Gift of Understanding, a complete disassociation, her seeing a younger me crawling up to this cliff, so young, so scared, my clothes bloodied, my only possessions fitting in a backpack. She's seeing me carve my name in the rocks because I want to be remembered. And I want to tell her it's not like that. That didn't happen. Her Gift of Understanding is steeped in selfish fear. But I can't because I am no longer a body or a voice. Her vision keeps going, working backward, me sleeping in my childhood bed, me creeping along the dead spots of the floorboards, me standing at the foot of my parents' bed, the same knife I'm now holding in my fifteen-year-old hand, tears and screams and the only voice of the powerless being gruesome violence, me enacting change the only way I knew how, my mantra being *love me love me leave me alone love me*. I want to tell Two to stop. I want to tell her Gifts of Understanding aren't True. They are intuition, but not Fact. I want to tell her that even if this did happen, the rest is True, but I am the powerless passenger to her connection to Truth, and then it's me stumbling along a road, dying of hypothermia, being picked up by the cops, questions being asked, arrests being made, the courts showing grace by naming me John Doe, juvie until I bashed my head into my cell wall and authorities deemed me worthy of CMHIP, a stumbled-upon book, a loose and broad narrative, the anonymous fifteen-year-old, John Doe to Mason Hues to Thirty-Seven, structure and doctrines to build a shattered life from, a loving family of my own choosing, acceptance, Dr. Turner always circling back to acceptance, to violence, to my father, Dr. Turner's progress destroyed when she pushed for a detail I didn't know, her asking about the DEA agents' bodies, and instead of the breakthrough she'd spent years working up to, I told her my name was Thirty-Seven.

I want to tell Two that what she sees isn't True. That I'd never lied to her. That I was Thirty-Seven. That I injected myself with three complete rounds of Cytoxan. That I'd pried teeth from severed heads. That I'd led a group because I was special, more dedicated, prized, a prophet.

I open my mouth. Two shakes her head. I crumple to the cave floor. I stare at the only woman I've ever loved. I let my whites be as vulnerable as possible. I strive for Honesty. I'm not sure what she sees. She reaches out her hand. I watch her eyes glass over as she pushes down the Gift of Understanding she's just experienced. She's doing everything we've worked so hard to eradicate. Her eyes swallow the vision. She will never be the same. She will never live in Honesty. She does this for love.

She extends her hand. She pulls me toward her. I tilt my head. She tells me she doesn't want to press foreheads. She pulls my head to her chest. I tell her everything happens for a reason. She says *don't*. I tell her it's not true. She pets my bald head. I tell her I'm so fucking sorry. She says she knows I am. I tell her it's not over, we can drive north, cross a completely unmanned boarder in the middle of Montana, start our lives over again, reinvent ourselves, live simply and Honestly, become anonymous. She tells me she'd like that. She presses her lips to my head. She says it again. "I'd like that." I don't look up because I know her eyes tell a different Truth.

# 46. THE DAY OF GIFTS[1]

The Andersons are new to Scottsdale. They've relocated from Kenosha, Wisconsin. Davis has a new job as a shift manager at Home Depot. Kristin has a new job working part-time at Talbots. Jenny is a sophomore and she's made varsity softball. Derek is in eighth grade. He wants to be a football player, but his fallback is being the CEO of Apple. They are amazed at the sun and the space and the highways five lanes wide. They live in a new development, originally planned for the upper middle-class, but after the recession, a half-finished home has become affordable. They are adjusting to a new climate and to new people, but they are doing it well, happy, together, family meals more often than not. They grill steaks on February tenth. They have a salad. Even though it's chilly by Arizona standards, they eat outside. The sun slips behind Camelback. They are content. They go to bed. They are butchered in their sleep. Everyone but thirteen-year-old Derek. He's held by the throat. He's forced to watch as a woman with no hair repeatedly plunges a knife into his mother and father's throat. He is instructed to lie by his sister as she bleeds out from a puncture wound in her vagina. Young Derek is told this is the greatest gift he will ever receive.

---

1 Reprinted in its entirety from O'Connor's *Dr. Sick: The Survivors and The Day of Gifts*

A man known by his followers as One slips into a home in Oklahoma City. He doesn't worry about fingerprints. He's not concerned about making noise. He holds a nine iron retrieved from the garage. He whistles. Amanda Bayle, seven years old, will later take to whistling this same tune a year later. She won't stop. Her new family, her aunt and uncle in Cleveland, will eventually identify the song as Elvis's "Blue Moon." But at that moment, she isn't sure if she's really hearing it or not. But she knows she hears screams. She hears the pleas for help. She hears her door open. A monster stands in her doorway. He is covered in blood. She screams. He extends his hands. He tells her it's okay. He tells her it was for her own good. She is too terrified to move. He holds her. Her family's blood drips from his chin to her face. He rocks her and calls her Zoe.

Andrew MacArthur awakes to a breaking of glass. He sits upright. His wife, Patricia, wakes as well, her first reaction checking the baby monitor where their newborn daughter sleeps. Andrew hears their kitchen door open. He reaches to his bedside table. His Colt .45 sits amidst change and condoms and an instructional manual to their new 3D television. He takes the pistol and climbs out of bed. He can hear someone at the end of their ranch-style home. He debates if he should call out to the intruder. He opts to stay silent. But then he hears the wails of his two-month-old baby. He runs. He bursts through the nursery door. He sees a woman cradling his baby. She looks possessed, not of this world, bald and dressed in black, a knife in her hand. The woman stares at Andrew as she slides the knife across his daughter's throat. Andrew screams and he fires his gun and bodies drop. His daughter is silent. His daughter will never cry again.

———

The Mendez family living in Springfield, Illinois, goes from six members to one in the span of seven minutes. The sole survivor, Andra Gabriella, mother of three, wife and daughter, watches as a man lines up her family in the living room. He makes them kneel. He holds an ax. Andra watches as he swings the blade into the heads of each person, oldest to youngest. Blood splatters against the painting of the Virgin Mary hanging on the wall. Andra Gabriella Mendez takes her life two days later.

Dennis Packer watches on as a man saws through the bones of his younger sister. She is still alive.

Reba Landry screams for help as she's dragged out from underneath her bed. A woman who looks like a ghost squats on her chest. The woman says, "I have killed everyone who would eventually betray you. I have done you a favor. I have given you a gift."

Tony Parker, only child, fourteen, bright but underachieving, plays World of Warcraft, when he hears screams coming from his parents' room. He takes off his earphones. He watches monsters on his screen kill one another. The screams intensify, both his mother and father, then his mother's become primal and his father's stop. Tony opens his window. He jumps ten feet to the backyard. He runs as fast as he can. Everything about the Chicago suburb appears foreign.

Four of the Smiths from Buckhead. Two Millers from Minneapolis. Three Brannons from Fresno. One Charles from Akron. Three Lanes from El Paso. Five Hendricksons from Fargo. Two Marshals from Olympia. Two Steins from St. Petersburg. Six Kellers from Lincoln. One Debauch from Bend. Three Rosenbergs from

Charleston. Two Mastersons from Denver. Five Yangs from Gary.
A single St. Michael from Tacoma. All dead. All butchered in vari-
ous forms of sleep. All leaving a single surviving family member.
Most of these survivors are told they were being given a gift.

A boy of fifteen makes a phone call. He's cold, sick from months of
undergoing chemotherapy. He stands at a bus station in Glenwood
Springs, Colorado. He calls 911.

"911, what's your emergency?"

"People are going to die."

"Excuse me?"

"Dr. James Shepard is behind it."

"Sir, are you in danger?"

"We're all in danger."

"What is your current location?"

"Truth."

"Sir, I need your name."

"Thirty-Seven."

"Your address? Thirty-seven what?"

"Gifts."[13]

---

13 I'm beyond fucked up reading this chapter. I'm sitting in Two's car.
We're at a rest stop. She's unconscious. We got her a bottle of gin because her pain was so severe. She drank and she drank and she drank. I
know it wasn't to actually stop the pain, but to stop Truth. She's unconscious and she's dying. And I don't know what the fuck to do. Where
the fuck to go. What the fuck is True. Her hand is swollen and red and
it's not bleeding anymore, but pussing, yellow and white, some of it
viscous, some like olive oil. She bleeds from the three dog bites. She
shakes in her sleep. I'm thinking about family members curled in the
same position and I'm thinking it's all bullshit and I'm thinking about
Dr. Turner's words the previous night—*you're not Thirty-Seven*—and
I'm picturing my father's three-year-old scars and I'm replaying Henry
O'Connor's accusation and I'm thinking about talking to the Feds, telling them stories, telling them exactly what's included in *Dr. Sick*, how

this is beyond a coincidence, and I'm thinking about my Reprieves with
Two, how they were different, stronger, darker than I'd experienced
around a fire, almost like it was new, DMT, all brand new. I'm sitting in
Dr. Turner's office. I'm holding *Dr. Sick*. I'm telling her it hadn't meant
to turn out that way. She's asking what wasn't supposed to turn out that
way. Violence. Death. Murder. She's asking me why I'm crying. I tell her
there are no accidents. She's asking me what happened that night. I tell
her I called the police. No, Mason, the night you ran away. I couldn't do
it. Couldn't do what? Kill anyone.

I'm granted a Gift of Understanding sitting at the rest stop.

It's our future, mine and Two's.

It's us in Canada. We've grown hair. We're older, early thirties. We
live in the country and we grow organic vegetables and we share an
old Chevy and we have learned how to yield sustainability from the
earth and we are tan. We are content. We sit around in front of our
cabin. I hear laughing. I look down and it's our son and he looks like
me and he's the second person in my life who has my own blood in his
veins. He jumps into my arms. Autumn is coming. Leaves are blushing.
Two—Talley—walks out of the house. She sees her two boys and she
smiles and she is beautiful and she is mine or I am hers or we are everyone's. She steps down the single step. Our son tells her she's getting fat.
I laugh, looking at Talley's belly. She is. There's another child in there. I
say, "Radiant." Talley says, "Bloated as hell." Our son says, "Hell." I roll
my eyes. Talley smiles. She wraps her arms around us and we watch the
sun set. We're anonymous. We're content. We're happy. We don't care
about sickness or Honesty or Truth.

Two's teeth chatter.

She's going to die. She won't be strong enough to trek into Canada.
She needs antibiotics and she needs stiches and she needs someone to
tell her *no*. That was her problem, her parents giving her everything,
thus everything becoming worthless, yes, yes, yes. I realize this is a gift I
can give. I can give her boundaries. I can save her life. I can take the rap
because it was my urging. I can face Truth.

And maybe this is the first Honest thing I've ever done, the first selfless act I've ever committed. And maybe this is unconditional love. And
maybe that's the only Truth there is.

I start driving to Florence.

I listen to "Blue Moon."

I drive up to the hospital's doors.

I press my forehead to Talley's. I tell her I love her more than
anything and that I'm sorry and that I don't know what's True and that

I want her to be happy, that's it, happy and loved, fulfilled, content, human.

I get out of the car.

I open the passenger's side door. I heave a passed-out Talley up against my body. I drag her to the curb. I am so gentle as I lay her head against the concrete. I am so gentle as I kiss her forehead, so fucking gentle.

# 47. DR. JAMES SHEPARD

I know One is imprisoned at the Florence ADX in Florence, Colorado. I know this because I wrote him a letter, addressed it and everything. Dr. Turner and I decided not to send it. She'd taken this act as progress.

It takes under two hours to get there.

I stop at Walmart and get civilian clothes. I change in the bathroom. I throw away my scrubs. I wash my face. I look like a memory. I won't meet my eyes in the mirror.

I need to know.

It's as simple as that.

I need to know the Truth. I need to know if I've made it all up, if everything I told Talley was bullshit, if I stabbed my father repeatedly, if I was more steeped in protective denial than any other American I'd been trying to change.

I drive to the prison. Everything around the compound is dead. The front building looks like a rec center to a semi-prosperous subdivision. There are fences fifteen feet high with razor wire and guard towers and barracks. I park the car. The sun beats down and things feel dry even though it's the middle of winter. I'm scared. I'm alone. I miss Talley and I miss my life and I miss my family and I miss Dr. Turner. I know that I will not walk out of this building. They will put two and two together, run a check on my name, pull me aside for questioning that feels a lot like interrogation.

But it doesn't matter.

I have nothing. I am nothing. I am Mason Hues. I am John Doe. I am One.

I get out of the car. I try my hardest not to look at the cameras hanging from parking lot light posts. I wear jeans and a white T-shirt. I limp a little. I reach the doors. My body is not my own. I walk inside. The smell is coffee and orange disinfectant. A woman security guard sits behind a blue desk. I want her to smile, but she doesn't. She stares at my baldness. It's all she sees. She asks what she can help me with and I tell her I'm here for visiting hours. She pulls out a sheet of paper and tells me to write down my name. *Mason Hues.* She asks for a driver's license. I tell her I don't have one. She asks for a social security card. I give her mine from my wallet. She writes a few numbers down. She tells me to step to the side. She tells me to tilt my chin back. She takes my picture. She prints it out on a visitor's nametag. She hands it to me. Our fingers touch, and I want this touch to mean something, but it's just an accident.

She asks the name of the prisoner I'm visiting.

"Dr. James Shepard."

Here the woman stops what she's doing. She looks at me, seeing me for the first time. The bald head suddenly makes sense. She's read *Dr. Sick.* She imagines her own family being butchered in their sleep. She sees me as a fellow Survivor. She nods. I know she'll inform those in the position to make people disappear when I leave her desk.

She tells me to take my first right, walk to the end of the hall, and I'll be admitted to the waiting room. I ask if it will take long. She glances at me from the corner of her eyes. The whites betray all of her intentions. I know it will take the rest of my life.

The echo of my feet is the same as it was in CMHIP.

Same with the electronic *thunk* of mechanized locks.

I walk into a small waiting room. There are two security guards behind a built-in desk and office. They stare at me as I sit. A little black kid rifles through his mother's purse. A TV hangs from the wall. It's tuned to old reruns of *The Andy Griffith Show*. There's no volume. The guards whisper and stare. I will invisibility. I will my body to disintegrate. I think about Talley being taken care of. I think about her feeling betrayed until she feels grateful. I will make it all go away. She will return to a life of normalcy. She'll be something close to happy. She won't talk about this portion of her life. It will be a piece of fabric in the quilt of her biggest regret, but it will be livable. I know the guards are looking at my record. They're either coming across a sealed file or one that says I tried to kill my father or one that says I was an accessory to seventy-seven counts of murder in the first degree.

"Hues."

I look up. A guard with the biggest dimple I've ever seen in a chin has opened the far door. He motions for me. I reach for a Gift of Understanding about where he's taking me but nothing comes. I meet his eyes for a split second as I walk past, and they are angry and disgusted and they are fearful.

We walk down a blue hallway. The walls are white. They feel as if they're constricting. I don't like having my back to the guard. I worry about billy clubs to the head or unzipped pants.

*Thunk.*

The door at the end of the hallway opens. He tells me to keep walking. I do. Then I'm in a long room, a corridor partitioned in two, stools and bulletproof glass and telephones, their twisted mirrored selves on the other side. The guard tells me to walk all the way to the end. I do. I can hardly breathe. I tell myself One will be happy to see me and that he'll know me and that he won't be mad about my snitching and that he'll stare at me and wonder who the fuck I am and what I want. I approach the end. I see orange and then I see an attractive man with a shaved head. One stares at me. I'm remembering everything—our talks on the boulder, our trip to Mexico, our sawing of the DEA agents, our foreheads pressing, One pressing his mouth to my ear and telling me his biggest regret was arriving at our particular Truth—and then I'm standing there unsure what to do.

I sit.

One stares.

I'm remembering countless nights in CMHIP where I stared at his picture in *Dr. Sick*. I'm remembering tracing my finger over the two-dimensional contours of his face. I'm remembering whispering to the pages, telling him my three, character-defining traits of Self.

I reach up to the phone hanging on the wall. My hand shakes. One looks at the cut in my palm. He takes a second to move, but then takes his receiver.

We don't talk.

I am terrified he won't know me; I'm terrified he will.

I don't want Truth. I want the deceit of arriving at Truth. I want to feel secure with my understanding of the world and myself and what happens when I commit atrocities and I want things to fit in boxes and I want Gifts of Understanding to be real instead of projections of how I see people's pasts and I want direction and rules and male love and to not have ever used a sharpened point to puncture skin.

His breath echoing in my ear is that of my father's, slightly labored, as if in pain, as he stands in my doorway.

"Do you know me?"

One stares at me. I want to shield the whites of my eyes and I want to be nothing but Truth.

One says, "I know everyone who has ever lived or ever will live."

"But me?"

"People who repeat questions know the Truth but want an answer that aids deceit."

I swallow.

"Just tell me...was I there?"

One says, "I can see it."

"Was I?"

"You have it."

"Have what?"

"My God," One says. He smiles. His left incisor is chipped. He seems to be in awe. "You possess Truth."

I shake my head.

"Judas denied possessing Truth."

"Please, just tell me if I was with you in Marble."

"It changes you. That's what people don't understand, you see. Truth. Once you've been exposed to it, it overtakes every aspect of your being."

I tell myself not to cry, but I can't help it.

"You remind me of someone," One says.

I remind him of Thirty-Seven because I've fashioned myself after an anonymous boy, the antihero of a loose and broad narrative.

"God," One says. He smiles.

"Do you know me? Please, just tell me if I was there in Marble. Tell me the Truth."

One looks over to his right. I turn to my left. The door at the end of the corridor opens and in walks another security guard, only he's different, dressed all in brown, a state trooper. He whispers to the guy who let me in. They stare. I turn back to One. He says, "They won't let you leave. That's the thing about those who arrive at Truth: they have to be removed from the populace. They have to be imprisoned. They have to be institutionalized. Because they can see it. Even if they don't understand what they're seeing, they see it. It clouds this whole fucking system. It makes every propagated *goal* inconsequential. It makes every consequence obsolete. It reminds them that one day they will die without any of the fanfare they believe they deserve."

I'm crying harder. I'm thinking about his bare chest as he shot the agents and I'm feeling his gentle touch as he punctured my skin with a needle full of Cytoxan and I'm standing at the foot of my parents' bed masturbating over my father and I'm alone in a locked cell with padded corners praying for any sort of companionship. I'm whispering *please* into the telephone.

One presses his index finger to the glass. He says, "You've given the world a gift. It will take them a while to understand it, but they will. And others will follow. You are a murmur, a tectonic hiccup, necessary before the quake that will change everything."

The door opens again. Another state trooper enters. I know they've run my name and I know my picture was captured in St. Paul and then again in the parking lot of CMHIP and our names were on the motel register in Pueblo and they saw me drop Talley off at the hospital and my blood is probably everywhere across this nation and it's over with and it's real even if it's not.

"Was I there?"

"You were everywhere," One says.

"I need to know."

"You already do."

The two troopers start down the corridor.

My voice gets louder. I'm begging him to tell me. He's smiling. They're getting closer. My vision is the first inhale of Reprieve and I'm pounding on the glass and wishing to turn back time to be lying in my bed with Talley and us in love with ideals and betterment and one another.

"There are no accidents," One says.

"Please."

"The only thing that's real is love and the loss of love."

"Do you know me?"

The troopers are at my side. They tell me to set the receiver down. I am granted a Gift of Understanding, and it's the future I've inflicted upon the rest of my family when I called the police or it's the future of strangers who'd murdered innocents.

"Hey," One says.

A trooper puts his hand on my shoulder. He pulls and squeezes. I yank my arm away, and this incites action, both guys grabbing me, and I struggle and scream, the receiver falling from my hand, my right arm twisted behind my body. There's a searing pain. All I hear is my father's screams and the burning of logs as we sit around a campfire and Elvis begging for protection. They shove my face against the counter. I crane my eyes so they meet One's, and there's sickness there. Honesty, Truth, pride, change, love, and he smiles, hanging up the receiver, and then he speaks to me and his words are silent, trapped behind alienating glass—*Welcome back, Thirty-Seven*—and the pain falls away and so does my body and I am only my mind and I am only consciousness and I am nothing and I never was and I have changed the world and I know all and I am God.